PO

# The Cattle Drive

# The Cattle Drive

## Ethan J. Wolfe

**FIVE STAR**
A part of Gale, a Cengage Company

Farmington Hills, Mich • San Francisco • New York • Waterville, Maine
Meriden, Conn • Mason, Ohio • Chicago

**LIBRARY OF CONGRESS CATALOGING-IN-PUBLICATION DATA**

Names: Wolfe, Ethan J., author.
Title: The cattle drive / Ethan J. Wolfe.
Description: First edition. | Farmington Hills, Mich.: Five Star, a part of Gale, Cengage Learning 2018.
Identifiers: LCCN 2017055244 (print) | LCCN 2017057438 (ebook) | ISBN 9781432840235 (ebook) | ISBN 9781432840228 (ebook) | ISBN 9781432838638 (hardcover)
Subjects: | BISAC: FICTION / Action & Adventure. | FICTION / Westerns. | GSAFD: Western stories. | Mystery fiction. | Suspense fiction.
Classification: LCC PS3612.A5433 (ebook) | LCC PS3612.A5433 C38 2018 (print) | DDC 813/.6—dc23
LC record available at https://lccn.loc.gov/2017055244

First Edition. First Printing: June 2018
Find us on Facebook–https://www.facebook.com/FiveStarCengage
Visit our website–http://www.gale.cengage.com/fivestar/
Contact Five Star™ Publishing at FiveStar@cengage.com

Printed in the United States of America
1 2 3 4 5 6 7 22 21 20 19 18

# The Cattle Drive

★ ★ ★ ★ ★

# The Runaways

★ ★ ★ ★ ★

# ONE

Angela Dunn kept busy by reading the booklet about the history of the Illinois Detective Agency, the largest and oldest agency of its type in the country. According to the booklet, the agency was founded thirty years earlier in 1850 by Frank Miller Sr., an immigrant from Ireland. He started the business with just three men besides himself and offered investigative services to the Chicago police and militia. His services were so in demand that even President Lincoln had used him on occasion. Within ten years the agency employed thirty men and by 1871, the year Miller passed away, it had grown to more than fifty agents in three major cities. They were Chicago, New York, and Boston. There were several more agencies of this type that had started up in the last decade, but the Illinois Detective Agency was the largest and most famous.

Frank Miller Jr. took the reins from his father and expanded the manpower to one hundred agents and added Philadelphia and San Francisco to the cities serviced by the agency. He had plans to add three additional cities in the next five years and create a coast-to-coast network of services available to law enforcement, the government, and the private citizen.

There were dozens of testimonials in the back of the booklet, including major newspaper headlines and a complete list of every agent's name, education, and work experience.

Angela set the booklet aside on an expensive-looking table in the plush waiting room. She stood up and went to look out a window. The view was dizzying, to be sure. The office was located on the top floor of a ten-story building, and she had never been so high above ground in her life. Past the street she could see Lake Michigan and all the boat traffic on the water. Sailboats occupied by couples, a paddleboat, rowboats, and even a large steamer or two.

"Mrs. Dunn?" a female voice behind Angela said.

Angela turned around. "Miss," she said. "I am unmarried."

"Pardon me," the woman said. "But Mr. Miller is ready to see you now."

Angela followed the woman from the waiting room and down a long hallway to an office that had a thick glass door. The words *Frank Miller Jr. President and Chief Executive* were etched in the glass and painted in gold.

The woman opened the door and escorted Angela into the spacious and very plush office. "Miss Angela Dunn," the woman said.

Frank Miller Jr. stood up from behind his large oak desk and came around to extend his right hand.

Angela took it and they shook hands for a moment.

"Miss Dunn, would you care for some coffee or tea?" Miller said.

"Tea would be my preference," Angela said.

Miller nodded to the woman, and she closed the door.

"Come sit at the conference table while I fix us tea," Miller said.

Angela walked to the table, which held ten chairs, and selected a chair so that her back was to a window.

Miller had a small hot-plate oven on a table in the corner of the room, fixed two cups of tea, and carried them to the table. He set one cup in front of Angela and then took a chair opposite her.

"Now, please tell me how I may be of service to you?" Miller said.

"I am the sole surviving heir of the Dunn family fortune," Angela said. "My sister and her husband passed away six months ago in a terrible boating accident on the lake. They were row-boating, and a steamer didn't see them."

"I do remember reading about that in the newspaper," Miller said. "I am truly sorry for your loss."

Angela sipped tea and studied Miller for a moment. He was around thirty-five or forty years old, and impeccably dressed in a wool suit, white shirt, and gold tie. He was tall with broad shoulders and reeked of confidence to the point of cockiness.

"It was a stupid accident that should never have happened," Angela said. "But happen it did, and it has left me in the predicament that has brought me to see you."

"How so?" Miller said.

"My sister left two children behind," Angela said. "Twins. Michael and Michele. They have been living with me the past six months but as I am unmarried, I am unable to give them a father figure in the household. I am afraid they have grown quite spoiled, as children of means are apt to do, and without a father's presence in the house I fear it will only grow worse."

"I understand completely," Miller said.

"My brother-in-law has a married sister living in San Francisco, and she and her husband have agreed to take the twins and raise them as their own," Angela said. "What I require from your agency is to transport the twins by railroad to San Francisco. Is this something that your agency is equipped to handle?"

"Certainly," Miller said. "We have done just such a task many times. I generally assign two men to escort the children, but given your standing and wealth, I think four men would be in order."

"I agree," Angela said. "The twins must be protected at all costs. How soon can you make the arrangements?"

"I will have my secretary check train schedules and make the reservations," Miller said. "Given the nature of this assignment, I will be part of the four-man team escorting the twins. Would three days be soon enough?"

"That would be fine," Angela said.

"I will drive out to your home tomorrow to review the details," Miller said. "If they meet with your approval, we will leave by railroad two days after that."

"Excellent. That gives me time to speak with the children," Angela said. "That also gives you the chance to get acquainted with Michael and Michele before the trip."

"Very good then," Miller said.

"One final thing," Angela said. "Don't spare the expense on this trip. I can well afford to pay top dollar to protect the children and make sure they are cared for in every way."

"Don't worry about a thing, Miss Dunn," Miller said. "The twins will be looked after as if they were my own."

# Two

Angela Dunn lived in the house her father had built in 1845 after he made the first of his fortune. Situated within walking distance of Lake Michigan and located ten miles outside the city limits of Chicago, it was the only residence she had ever known in her forty-two years of living.

Designed with the affluence her father earned in steel, the home and property on the shores of the lake cost an astounding eighty thousand dollars to build, an unheard-of sum of money thirty-five years before when she was just a child. Recent estimates by appraisers valued the house and property at five times its original cost, a staggering sum indeed.

When her father died ten years ago, he left his fortune of nineteen million dollars, split equally between Angela and her younger, more frivolous sister, Abigail. Abigail chose to do nothing with her fortune except spend it and spoil her husband and children. Angela chose to become part of her father's empire, and within five years tripled her inheritance.

She was a cold and calculating businesswoman, having learned at her father's knee the steel business and his skill at investments and profits and, most importantly, in dealing with the competition.

Angela had little time for suitors, had never married, and doubted she ever would. Even though she employed a staff of six and hired a nanny and tutor for the twins, she knew she couldn't give them what they really needed, a loving family and a father figure in the home.

A mother who would guide and shuffle them into adulthood without sparing the rod, and a father to provide family leadership and values. She lacked both and could do neither.

She broke the news to them at dinner.

Michael wore a suit, tie, and short pants to the formal dining table.

Michele wore a stylish dress suited for summer dining. Her long blond hair was in a French braid that no doubt took the nanny several hours to prepare.

"Three weeks on a train?" Michael said.

"That's how long it will take to go from Chicago to San Francisco, because you will make many stops and change trains for security purposes," Angela said.

"I don't understand why we can't stay with you," Michele said.

"I've already told you why," Angela said. "You need a real family environment to grow up in, and I can't give you that. Your aunt in San Francisco has a husband and two children of about your age, and moving you there will be much better all the way around for everybody concerned."

"For everybody or just you?" Michele said.

"That will be quite enough of your smart mouth, young lady," Angela said.

"Why can't you just get a husband?" Michael said. "Then we could stay and be yours."

"I'm far too busy to marry, I'm afraid," Angela said. "And besides, I'm sure once you get there and are settled in you will much prefer living in San Francisco than in Chicago."

"All we know is Chicago," Michael said.

"Then you'll soon have the opportunity to know more," Angela said.

"What about all our things?" asked Michele.

"I've hired a freight company to pack all your clothing, books, and personal items into crates, and they will deliver them to the railroad yard," Angela said. "Your things will arrive in San Francisco when you do."

"Yes, ma'am," Michele said.

"Now finish your dinner," Angela said. "We have much to prepare for this trip."

"I'm going to run away," Michael said. "That's what I'm going to do."

"No, you're not," Michele said. "Because if you run away, then I have to run away, and I don't want to."

They were in Michele's bedroom, a spacious room with a canopy bed that was large enough to hold all of her dolls and satin-wrapped pillows.

"I'm not asking you to go," Michael said. "I'm a boy, and boys are better at running away than girls."

"Says who?" Michele said.

"Says everybody. Boys know how to do things that girls don't, such as hunt and make fires and find water in the desert. Girls can't do any of that."

"In the books you've read, you can do those things," Michele said. "Neither of us has ever left Chicago and, to tell you the truth, I don't want to leave."

"Well, we have no choice," Michael said. "That's why I'm running away the first chance I get. When no one is looking, I'm jumping off the train."

Michele sat on her bed and started to sniffle. "Don't you even think about running away without taking me," she said.

"Aw, jeeze, Mikey," Michael said. "I can't run away and have you crying."

"You promise me right now, Mickey," Michele said. "Go on and promise."

"Promise what?"

"That if you run away, you won't leave me behind."

Michael sighed. "Okay."

"Say it."

"Jeeze, Mikey."

"Say it or I'll punch you in the nose."

"I'll punch you back."

"You can't punch me back. I'm a girl."

"Then I'll pull your hair."

"No you won't, either. Pull my hair, and I'll kick you a good one in the shin. Now promise."

Michael sighed openly, defeated.

"Okay, I promise that if I run away I'll take you with me."

Michele spat on her hand and looked at Michael. "Spit," she said.

Michael spat on his right hand and they shook on the promise.

"If you break your promise, God will punish you," Michele said.

"God has better things to do," Michael said.

"Maybe, but he sees everything," Michele said. "Sit."

Michael sat on the bed and Michele put her head on his shoulder.

"Being your brother is no picnic in Chicago Park," Michael said.

# THREE

Frank Miller proved to be a man of his word and arrived at the Dunn mansion fully prepared at ten in the morning.

Angela received Miller in her expansive den where she introduced him to the twins.

"Michael and Michele," Angela said.

"Pleased to meet you, and rest assured you two that my men and I will guard you with our lives," Miller said.

"Are you married?" Michael said.

"My wife is deceased," Miller said.

"What's that?" Michael said.

Michele whispered into Michael's ear.

"Then you can marry my aunt so we don't have to leave," Michael said.

"That is quite enough out of you, Michael," Angela said.

"Yes ma'am," Michael said.

"It's perfectly all right," Miller said. "Let me show you the railroad route I've chosen for their safety."

Miller spread out a large map of the states and territories on the wide table.

"I mapped out the best, safest route in red pencil," he said. "From Chicago we travel west on a local train until we reach Medicine Bow, Wyoming. The train makes several key stops along the way and the journey will take three days' time. In Medicine Bow we switch to the Western Pacific and travel through Utah and Nevada. In Nevada we have a layover of one day. Then we travel directly into San Francisco without any stops. The total travel time is eight days and nights and, considering the first part of the trip is aboard a local train, that is excellent time. I had thought two weeks or more, but my planner mapped out this route."

"Eight days and nights on a train!" Michael said.

"You hush, Michael," Angela said.

"It won't be that bad, son," Miller said. "There is a great deal to see traveling by train, and there is a game car where you can play checkers and chess or read books. And the food on board is quite good, I assure you."

"Where do we sleep?" Michael said.

"You have a first-class suite with two bedrooms, a living room, and a private toilet," Miller said. "You can even have a bath."

"Any more questions children?" Angela said.

"No, ma'am," Michael said.

"Then go finish with the freight company," Angela said. "I have some private business to discuss with Mr. Miller."

Michael and Michele left the den and closed the door.

"About your bill?" Angela said.

"I pride myself on a fair deal, Miss Dunn," Miller said. "I charge by the hour. Fifteen dollars per hour for each man. Total hours should be between five hundred seventy-six and six hundred, depending upon the on-time record at the switch points and escort service to and from the home and in San Francisco. Roughly nine thousand dollars plus expenses."

"That can't be right," Angela said. "You said four men."

"I never charge for myself," Miller said. "That's also my firm policy."

"What about expenses?"

"I think two thousand will cover all meals, sundries, and whatnot," Miller said. "All expenditures will be itemized and with receipts when possible, with notes when not, and all non-used expense money will be returned to you upon my return to Chicago."

"I must admit that I had reservations about this, but you have put them all to rest," Angela said. "Thank you."

"The agency wouldn't have lasted for thirty years and have the reputation we do if we didn't live up to our promises," Miller said.

"Would you like the expense money in cash or check?" Angela said.

"Either is fine," Miller said. "I won't submit the final bill until the twins are safely in the hands of their new caretakers and I return to Chicago."

"I'll write you a check for the expenses then," Angela said.

"Thank you," Miller said.

"No, thank you, Mr. Miller," Angela said. "This is a very big load off my mind. A very big load indeed."

# FOUR

Michael, Michele, and Angela waited in front of the mansion. Two servants stood back a bit with three heavy crates. Michael and Michele each held a carry-on tote bag filled with personal items and sundries.

Miller arrived with three of his agents five minutes before the agreed-upon time of ten in the morning. There were two carriages. One carriage for the crates and the other for the twins.

Miller stepped down from his carriage.

"Good morning, Miss Dunn, Michael, and Michele," Miller said. "It's a fine morning for traveling."

"Good morning to you, Mr. Miller," Angela said.

"These are my associates, Mr. Tiller, Mr. Deeds, and Mr. Pep, all experienced agents and hand-picked by myself for this job," Miller said.

"Good morning to you all," Angela said.

"Come, lads, and get those crates loaded," Miller said. "We have a train to catch, and it won't wait on us if we're late."

As Deeds, Tiller, and Pep loaded the crates onto the second wagon, Angela pulled Miller aside to speak in private.

"Mr. Miller, I notice that you are wearing a suit," Angela said. "May I ask if you and your men are armed?"

Miller opened his suit jacket to reveal a Colt revolver in a shoulder holster.

"We believe it puts people at ease if they don't see firearms in plain sight on a train," Miller explained. "My men and I are experts with a long rifle and handgun if and when the need be. We have Winchester rifles packed in special cases."

"I pray it won't be necessary for that expertise to be demonstrated at any time on this trip," Angela said.

"I expect this trip to be smooth sailing from start to finish, but rest assured that we will protect the twins with our very lives if it is necessary to do so," Miller said.

"Loaded up, Mr. Miller," Deeds said.

"Allow me a moment to say goodbye to the twins," Angela said.

Michael and Michele sat inside the coach while Miller and Deeds drove the horses from atop on the driver's platform.

As they watched their aunt fade from their view through the window, Michele started to cry softly.

"Are you going to cry like a girl the whole time?" Michael said.

"I am a girl, and I'll cry all I want," Michele said.

Michael sighed and looked out the window. "It won't be so bad," he said. "I bet San Francisco is a real nice place. You won't miss Chicago hardly at all."

"You are so stupid, Michael," Michele said. "It's not Chicago I'll miss. I'll miss Mom and Dad. They are buried here and I won't be able to visit them anymore. I'll miss our school and my room and all of our friends."

Michael pulled out his pocket handkerchief and gave it to Michele.

"Wipe your nose," Michael said.

Michele dabbed her eyes and then blew her nose.

"Thank you," she said.

Michael nodded and then looked out the window so that Michele wouldn't see the mist forming in his eyes.

"You're welcome," he said with a quivering lower lip.

# FIVE

The railroad station was the loudest, dirtiest and most exciting place Michael and Michele had ever seen. The majestic interior of the main building was lavishly decorated with a large, four-faced clock centered in the room. People rushed to and fro at an alarming rate. They saw for the first time a person dressed in rags with a tin cup, begging for money.

On the platforms, trains were everywhere. Whistles blew, steam engines hissed, men shouted as cargo and passengers were loaded. It was all so confusing just standing and watching it all.

Miller and his men escorted them onto a train he said was theirs. They followed him through several cars to their suite.

"This is home for the next eight days," Miller said. "Pick a room for each of you. I'll leave Mr. Tiller to watch over you while I check us in. I won't be long."

Miller closed the door and left them alone with Tiller.

Michele opened a door to one bedroom. "This one is mine," she said and tossed her bag onto the bed.

Michael opened the door to the other bedroom and placed his bag on the bed. "Mr. Tiller, where do . . ."

"My friends call me Frog," Tiller said. "You may call me that if you like."

Michael and Michele returned to the living room.

"Frog?" Michele said. "That's a funny name."

"Why do they call you that?" Michael said.

"Why do you think?" Tiller said.

Michael looked at Tiller and noticed that the man's eyes seemed to bulge right out of his face.

"Your eyes," Michael said. "They stick out like the eyes on a frog."

Tiller laughed. "Yes, they do," he said. "I have this condition the docs call proptosis. It makes my eyes bulge out like a frog. It doesn't hurt me none and I see just fine, so if you want to call me Frog, you just go right ahead. It's what all my friends call me, and I take no insult in the name."

"Mr. Frog, I was wondering where Mr. Miller and you sleep," Michael said.

"Next door and across the hall," Tiller said. "He has it worked out so two men share night watch from the room across the hall so we can watch your door all night."

A whistle blew outside the train.

"That's us," Tiller said. "We'll be leaving the station in a few minutes."

"Mr. Frog, I'm hungry," Michele said. "It was a very long drive to the train."

"I'm a bit hungry, too," Tiller said. He pulled out his pocket watch and checked the time. "I do believe the eating car opens one hour after we leave the station. We'll get a bite to eat then."

The door suddenly opened and Miller, Deeds, and Pep entered the stateroom.

"All checked in," Miller said. "So what do you twins want to do? Ride in the passenger car and watch the countryside, go to the library car and read or play checkers, or stay here?"

"When the eating car opens, we want lunch," Michael said.

"And then visit the library car," Michele said.

"Good plan," Miller said. "Some food will do us all some good."

★ ★ ★ ★ ★

The dining car was as ornate and fancy as any restaurant the twins had ever visited with their parents in Chicago, and they had visited a great many. Their parents were well known about town as socialites.

Michael and Michele sat at a table with Miller. Deeds, Pep, and Frog, as they now thought of the bug-eyed man, occupied the table directly behind them so both doors to the car could be watched at the same time, Miller explained.

Michele ordered baked chicken. Miller asked for a bloody steak, and Michael, copying Miller, ordered the same.

Dessert was a choice of cake, pie, or cookies with milk, tea, or coffee.

After lunch, Miller and Frog took the twins to the library car. Michele read a book from the expansive library. Michael played several games of checkers with Frog.

Then suddenly the train slowed, the whistle blew several times, and they stopped.

"Water stop," Miller said.

"What's that?" Michael said.

"The train needs to take on water and coal or wood for the steam engine to run," Miller explained. "The whole thing runs on steam, so there will be a number of such stops along the way."

Michael and Michele went to the window. There was a giant water barrel on a tower the train stopped beside. Several men positioned a long flume to the water tank on the train and filled it with water.

"Sometimes when they take on water and coal, they allow passengers off to stretch a bit," Miller said.

Within ten minutes the water tank was full, and they were on their way again.

"Mr. Miller, can I take this book to my room?" Michele said.

"I'll go with you," Miller said.

"What about you?" Frog said to Michael.

"Can we play another game?" Michael said.

"Okay, but just one more," Frog said. "A grown man can stand only so much of getting beat by a little boy."

After Miller and Michele left the library, Michael made the first move on the checkerboard.

"It's your move, Mr. Frog," Michael said.

That evening, while Michael played checkers in the stateroom with Frog and Michele read a book in her bed, the train came to another water stop.

"I counted seven water stops so far," Michael said.

"You'll probably count twenty more before we reach Medicine Bow," Frog said.

"Mr. Frog, what's in Medicine Bow?" Michael said.

"Don't rightly know," Frog said. "Never been there. If the railroad built a station there, the place must have something. A lot of cattle would be my guess. I guess we'll find that out when we get there."

Michael nodded. "It's your move," he said.

# Six

One day's ride outside of Medicine Bow, Michael and Michele were looking forward to getting off the train to stretch their legs and walk around a bit during the several hours of layover time.

After dinner, while Miller and Pep occupied the car across from the twin's stateroom, Michael and Michele were getting ready for bed in their bedrooms. Michele discovered that her water pitcher was empty.

"Mickey, can you get me some water," Michele said.

"Why can't you get it yourself?" Michael said.

"I'm in my nightclothes," Michele said. "It wouldn't be proper for me to be seen walking around the hall by others in my nightclothes."

"All right," Michael said. "But it's a poor excuse if you ask me."

Michele handed Michael her empty water pitcher through the door.

"Ask if they could get ice," Michele said.

"Maybe you'd like some lemonade or buttermilk to go with it?" Michael said.

"Mickey, shut up and get the water," Michele said and closed her door.

Michael walked to the front door of the stateroom. "Just because she was born two minutes before me, she thinks she's the boss," he muttered.

At the door, Michael slowly opened it and peered into the

hallway. Directly across from him, the door to Mr. Miller's room was slightly ajar. Soft voices filtered into the hallway from the crack in the door.

Michael stepped out and was about to knock on the door when he heard Mr. Miller speak.

"When we reach Medicine Bow tomorrow afternoon, we'll pass the twins off to the boys and then wire Chicago they've been kidnapped," Miller said. "One or two of us will have to take a bullet to make it look good. Maybe in the arm or leg, but nothing serious. We'll pursue our boys for a few days and then wire Dunn with the ransom demands from Laramie. I think five hundred thousand per brat is a nice number."

"That woman is worth a hell of a lot more than that, Frank," Pep said. "She's the richest woman from Chicago to New York. I say seven hundred and fifty thousand for each kid is more like it."

"What do you say, Frog?" Miller said.

"I think Pep is right," Frog said. "She can well afford to pay that amount and then some."

"I'll consider it. Go get Deeds," Miller said. "He'll need to hear the entire plan."

Michael backed into the stateroom and slowly closed the door. He held his breath as he heard Deeds leave Miller's room and the door closed.

Then Michael tiptoed to Michele's room and softly knocked on her door.

"Mikey, open the door, it's me," Michael said.

The door jerked open. "You're back awful quick to . . ."

Michael shoved Michele into her room and shut the door.

"What's the big—?" Michele said.

"Quiet," Michael said.

"This is my room and I'll . . ." Michele said.

Michael put his hand over her mouth.

"I told you to be quiet," Michael said. "I heard something in the hallway."

"You're a big fat liar, Michael," Michele said.

"No I'm not either, and keep your voice down," Michael said. "They'll hear us talking and come in, and then we'll be in a real fix."

"What you said is crazy talk, Michael," Michele said. "Aunt Angela is paying them to protect us, not kidnap us."

"He called it ransom money," Michael said. "Seven hundred and fifty thousand dollars for each of us, and that's a lot more than she's paying them to protect us."

"Are you making this up, Michael?" Michele said. "Tell me the truth."

"No, I am not making it up."

"Swear."

"I swear I'm not making this up."

"Swear on Mom and Dad."

"I swear on Mom and Dad I am not making this up."

Michael slowly sat on Michele's bed.

"We're in trouble, Mickey."

"Looks that way."

"What are we going to do?" she said.

"Jump off the train," Michael said.

"What are you talking about?" Michele said. "The train is going faster than a horse can run. We'll get killed if we jump off the train."

"Not if we wait for a water stop and sneak out the window," Michael said. "There should be at least two more stops before we reach Medicine Bow. When the train stops, we'll jump off when it's not moving. Now get dressed."

Michele stared at Michael.

"I'm scared, Mickey," she said.

"You'll be a whole lot more scared if we let them kidnap us," Michael said. "Now get dressed—and no dresses. Your legs will get all cut up."

"Well, what am I supposed to wear? All I have are dresses. I'm a girl."

"I have extra pants. Wear those."

"Pants?" Michele said. "I can't wear pants. That wouldn't be proper."

"Suit yourself, but when your proper legs are all cut up and bleeding don't . . ."

"All right, I'll wear pants."

"And one of my shirts," Michael said. "Now hurry up and change. We don't want to miss the water stop."

Fifteen minutes later, dressed alike in dark trousers and shirts, Michael and Michele waited in her bedroom for the train to stop for water.

"Michael, where are we supposed to go?" Michele said. "When we jump off the train, I mean. We can't just wander around. We don't know where we are or where to go."

"We can't go west, because that's where they're going," Michael said. "They will probably look for us east along the tracks, so we best go north or south and look for a farmhouse or something. There's bound to be some people living around here who can help us."

"What about food and water?"

"I have some candy and a bottle of pop."

"Wait, I have some chocolate bars in my bag."

"We'll load everything into one bag and take that," Michael said.

"Okay."

"I'll grab my satchel."

After loading the satchel, Michael and Michele sat on the

bed and waited for the next water stop.

Finally, after what seemed like a very long time, Michele said, "I think the train is slowing down. Get ready."

# Seven

Michael cracked open the window in the bathroom. Fully open, it wasn't wide enough for an adult to squeeze through, but someone his size would have no problem getting out.

He watched as the train rolled to a stop and the workers went about filling the water tank from the tower.

"Now," he whispered to Michele. "And be very quiet."

"I'm scared, Mickey."

"Don't you cry. Now is not the time for crying."

"I'm not crying," Michele said. "I said I was scared, and that's not the same thing as crying."

"I'm just as scared as you," Michael said. "Now come on. I'll go first, and you throw me the bag."

Michael wiggled headfirst out of the window, took hold of the side of the car with his hands, pulled himself all the way out, and stood on the edge of the window. It was about a four-foot drop to the ground, and on a silent count of three he jumped.

Michael landed in the dirt beside the tracks, rolled over, and stood up.

"Nothing to it," he whispered. "Toss me the bag."

Michele tossed the bag to Michael, and he set it beside him on the ground.

"Now you—and hurry," Michael said. "They're almost done filling the water tank."

Michele wiggled out of the window and stood on the edge.

"Michael, I'm afraid," she whispered.

"Would you jump already," Michael whispered.

"I can't," Michele said.

"They're through loading the water," Michael said.

"I can't do it, Michael," Michele said.

A whistle blew. The engine came to life, and the greased wheels started to slowly turn and inch the massive train forward.

"Now! Jump now!" Michael said.

"Catch me," Michele said.

"I can't catch you unless you jump."

The train started to pick up speed, and Michael had to run alongside the tracks.

"Now!" Michael yelled.

Michele closed her eyes and jumped off the edge of the window.

She landed on top of Michael and they fell backward and rolled to safety. The train picked up speed and roared past them.

"Are you hurt?" Michael said.

"I don't think so."

"Then let's go."

Michael and Michele stood up. Michael grabbed the bag and, as the train raced along the tracks, he took Michele's hand and they ran into the darkness.

"Michael, slow down," Michele said. "I can't walk another step."

Michael stopped and released Michele's hand.

"We haven't gone far enough yet," Michael said. "I heard a train whistle."

"It's miles away," Michele said. "It's just so loud you can still hear it, is all."

"Let's sit on that big rock over there," Michael said and pointed.

They walked to the rock and took seats.

"Where are we?" Michele said.

"I don't know. Wyoming, I think."

"The moon is up now," Michele said. "And look at all those stars. We never see stars like this in Chicago."

"Never mind the stars," Michael said. "We need to figure out where we are and where we're going."

"We need to find a farm or a house or something," Michele said. "Some place with people who can help us."

"Well, we're not going to find that sitting here on this stupid rock," Michael said.

"Michael, stop," Michele said. "I'm so tired and my feet hurt."

"I'm tired, too," Michael said. "Just a little bit more."

"No," Michele said and yanked her hand free of Michael's. "I can't walk another step. I'm tired and my feet hurt."

"All right," Michael said. "I guess we've gone far enough for one night."

"They won't even know we're gone until breakfast," Michele said.

"Maybe we can find a place to sleep?"

"Where?"

"I don't know," Michael said. "On the ground someplace I guess."

"On the ground? With bugs and such?"

"Do you see any nice soft beds with pillows and dolls around here?" Michael said. "We can use the satchel for a pillow."

"Where?"

"Anywhere. Right here is good."

Michele and Michael got down on their backs and used the satchel as a pillow. It was uncomfortable, but it would have to do for the night.

They were silent for a few minutes, but it was obvious that neither of them was asleep.

"Michael, I'm cold," Michele said.

"Go to sleep."

"I can't, I'm cold," Michele said. "I can't sleep if I'm cold."

"Well, what do you want me to do about it?"

"Hug me for warmth," Michele said.

"I'm not going to . . ."

"I'm freezing, Mickey. Now hug me."

"All right already. Jeez."

Michele placed her head against Michael's chest and he wrapped his arms around her. "Don't you tell anybody about this," he said. "About me hugging you I mean."

"Who am I going to tell, the kidnappers?" Michele said.

"We need to find a farmhouse or something in the morning," Michael said.

"In the morning," Michele said. "Right now I'm tired."

"So go to sleep."

"I will if you shut up."

"I'll shut up if you go to sleep."

Hugging his sister tightly, Michael closed his eyes, and the two of them slowly drifted into an exhausted, dreamless sleep.

# EIGHT

"What time do you think it is?" Michele said.

"I don't know," Michael said. "Around eight in the morning I figure."

"Where do you think we are?"

"Miles from the railroad is all I know," Michael said. "Let's eat something and get going. We need to find a farmhouse or something and telegraph Aunt Angela."

Michele opened the satchel.

"We have four chocolate bars, some hard candy, and a bottle of pop," she said.

"We'll have one chocolate bar now and half the pop and save the rest for later," Michael said. "Maybe we can find some water on the way."

They ate half a chocolate bar each and drank half the pop. The bottle had a cork, and Michael was careful to replace it just so to make sure none of it spilled when they packed up the satchel.

"Okay, let's go," Michael said.

"Which way?"

Michael looked at the sun. In school they were taught how to tell direction by the placement of the sun in the sky.

"That way is east. We can't go that way," he said. "North takes us back to the railroad tracks, and we can't go that way either. We'll go south and look for a farmhouse with some people who maybe will give us a real breakfast."

"Mickey, do you think they know we're gone by now?" Michele said.

"Yeah."

"They'll come after us, won't they?"

"Not yet they won't," Michael said. "Come on."

Pep and Deeds were in the room opposite the twins. They had the door open and were drinking coffee when Miller and Frog stopped by.

"We're going to breakfast," Miller said. "Wait a half hour and bring the brats to the dining car. We reach Medicine Bow in four hours, so it might be their last hot meal for a while. Ours, too."

"Okay, Frank," Deeds said.

"Michael, slow down," Michele said. "I can't walk as fast as you."

"I'm trying to find a place to stay," Michael said.

"I know, but my feet hurt."

"Look," Michael said and pointed to the sky.

Michele looked up at the ugly dark clouds forming overhead.

"It's going to rain," Michele said.

"And soon," Michael said. "We need to find a place to hide or get soaked."

"You smell something?" Pep said as he looked out the window.

"Yeah, rain," Deeds said. "It's time to get them kids up."

"I'll do it," Pep said.

Pep crossed the hall and knocked on the stateroom.

"Hey you two, come on to breakfast," Pep said.

There was no response.

"Hey in there, let's go," Pep said and banged on the door.

After a few seconds of silence, Pep grabbed the door handle, turned it, and pushed the door open.

The sky darkened so much, it was almost like night. Then lightning flashed, thunder boomed, and the hard rain started to fall almost in sheets.

"Michael, we're going uphill," Michele gasped.

"I know that," Michael said. "We're heading for that thick clump of bushes over there for some cover. See?"

Dragging Michele by the hand, Michael led her to the top of the hill where a large, very thick clump of bushes was bunched tightly together.

Michael broke some branches and made an opening.

"Get in," he said.

"It's full of thorns," Michele said.

"Do you want to get scratched or soaked?" Michael said. "Use the satchel to make a hole we can crawl into."

Holding the satchel in front of her, Michele pushed her way into the opening until there was room enough for two. Michael followed and they sat on the dirt as the rain started to fall even harder.

The lightning and thunder continued, and the rain came down with the force of hail, but the roof of thick bushes held fast.

"It worked," Michael said. "It's not leaking."

Lightning flashed again, booming thunder echoed, and Michele hugged Michael and closed her eyes.

"Boy, I'll bet that Mr. Miller is really surprised, huh?" Michael said.

"I don't think surprised is the right word," Michele said.

Miller and Frog crashed into the stateroom.

"Don't tell me they're gone!" Miller yelled.

Pep and Deeds looked at Miller.

"How could they be gone?" Miller said.

"Bathroom window is open," Pep said. "They must have jumped out during the night. Maybe at that last water stop."

Miller, his face twisted in anger, turned to Deeds and Pep.

"You were supposed to guard the brats all night," Miller said. "Were you sleeping?"

"No, we wasn't sleeping," Deeds said.

"We sat up all night with our door open so we could see their door," Pep said. "It never opened. How was we supposed to know they'd jump out the window? We never went into their bedrooms. We didn't have cause for that."

Miller sighed. "They must have found out about our plan somehow."

"How?" Pep said.

"I don't know," Miller said. "Maybe they heard us talking through the door? That doesn't matter now. They're gone, and we have to get them back pretty damn quick."

"Well, what do we do now?" Frog said.

"We go after them!" Miller shouted. "What do you think? We'll get horses in Medicine Bow and backtrack them. How far could two kids on foot get even with a twelve-hour head start?"

"What if they got picked up somehow?" Frog said.

"Then we'll take them back from whoever picked them up," Miller said. "Any way we can."

"I think the rain is stopping," Michele said.

"Are you wet?" Michael said.

"A little. Not much."

Michael peered out through the opening in the brush to discover it was not nearly as dark as it had been a few minutes ago.

"It's getting light," he said. "We should get going."

Michael tossed the satchel out first and then crawled out of the brush and stood up. Michele quickly followed. She looked at her clothes and picked thorns out of them.

"We're on a hill," Michele said. "Where do we go?"

"Down."

"I meant direction."

"Does it matter?"

"I guess not."

Michael picked up the satchel, and together they walked to the edge of the hill and started down the other side.

The hill was steep, the grass was wet, and it was difficult to keep their balance. After twenty feet or so, the grass thinned out and Michael and Michele found themselves walking in mud. Very slippery mud.

"Mickey?" Michele said from behind Michael.

"What?"

Michele slipped onto her back and slid past Michael, knocking him down. Together they slid three hundred feet to the bottom of the hill, twisting, turning, and rolling before they came to a stop at the bottom.

Covered in mud from head to toe, the twins sat up and looked at each other.

"Are you hurt?" Michael said.

"I'm covered in mud," Michele said.

"I know, but are you hurt?"

"I don't think so."

"Let's get out of here," Michael said. "Maybe we can find a stream to wash off."

Michele attempted to stand and immediately slipped and fell.

Michael somehow made it to his feet and held his hand out to Michele. She took it, and he pulled her to her feet.

"My hair is disgusting," Michele said. "And my fingernails are filthy."

"We'll find a stream," Michael said. "Remember geography

class. Water runs downhill. All we have to do is look for a stream running downhill."

"We just ran downhill and I didn't see any stream," Michele said. "All I saw was mud in my face."

"Let's go," Michael said.

Miller and Frog entered the Lucky Star Saloon in Medicine Bow shortly after one in the afternoon.

Houle and Ferris were at a table waiting for them. Hard men, outlaws really, Houle and Ferris were often employed by Miller for jobs out west that required a less-than-delicate touch. Both men were willing to use their guns, if the money was to their liking and the law wasn't around to witness it.

"Problem," Miller said as he took a seat at the table.

Frog went to the bar for two shots of whiskey and carried them to the table, where he gave one shot to Miller.

"The brats jumped the train during the night," Miller said. "We need four horses and you two to come with us and track them down."

"They jumped the train?" Houle said. "I thought you said they were just twelve-year-old kids?"

"They are," Miller said. "They jumped out a window at a water stop. They must have found out somehow about our plan."

"That rain must have washed out any tracks them kids made," Ferris said. "How are we supposed to find them?"

"They're kids alone without food and water. How far do you think they'll get on foot?" Miller said. "Finish your drinks and let's move out. Frog, get a week's supplies at the general store. We'll meet at the livery in thirty minutes."

"Michael, I'm tired," Michele said. "We've been walking in the hot sun for hours and we—"

"There!" Michael shouted and pointed to a hill. "A stream."

Michael grabbed Michele's hand and yanked her forward. They ran about a hundred yards to the base of a tall hill, where a fresh water stream flowed into a shallow but wider river.

"It doesn't look too deep," Michael said. "We can just jump in and wash off this mud."

"Jump in with our clothes on?" Michele said.

"We could wait for Aunt Angela's laundry maid to show up and wash them for us," Michael said.

"No need to get smart-mouth with me," Michele said.

Michael sat down and removed his shoes. "Take your shoes off first," he said. "We'll need to keep them dry."

Michele sat and took off her shoes.

"We don't have any soap," Michele said.

"The mud will wash off anyway," Michael said. "It's just mud. Are you ready?"

"No."

"I'll go first," Michael said.

Michael and Michele stood up, and slowly Michael stepped off the embankment and into the very cold water. He walked out to the center of the stream where it was about three feet deep.

"Is it cold?" Michele said.

"Warm as a bath," Michael said. "Jump in."

Michele stood at the edge of the embankment, lifted her hands over her head, and dove into the stream they way they taught her in swim class at the private school.

She came up for air screaming.

"It's freezing, Michael!" Michele shouted. "You lied to me."

"Don't be such a big baby," Michael said. He dove under, and when he came up he said, "At least we're clean."

Miller and his five men met at the livery corral. Frog had an extra horse loaded down with supplies.

"After we pick up the brats, we'll continue the plan as scheduled," Miller said. "I'd like to make that last water spot by late afternoon. Maybe they got off there. It shouldn't be too hard to pick up their tracks, even with that rain."

"What about the rest of our boys?" Ferris said. "We promised them a payday."

"Let them stay in town and get drunk for a few days," Miller said. "If six of us can't find two kids on foot, we're a sorry bunch. Let's ride."

Michael and Michele sprawled out on the side of the hill to let the warm afternoon sun dry their clothes.

The heat of the sun and exhaustion from walking took its toll on them, and it wasn't long before they fell asleep.

After an hour or so, a noise stirred Michele and she slowly opened her eyes. Beside her Michael was still sleeping, so the noise didn't come from him.

Michele closed her eyes again and a moment later the noise sounded a second time.

It sounded almost like a . . . baby rattle.

But that would be ridiculous. They were in the middle of nowhere, alone and . . .

The rattle sounded again.

Michele opened her eyes and turned her head to the left. There on the rocks about four feet away was a long, very angry rattlesnake. Its rattle-like tail was high in the air and it shook violently at her.

Michele jumped up screaming. Immediately Michael woke and jumped up beside her. They looked at the deadly snake and screamed together.

The snake flicked its tongue at them, and then slowly slithered away into the rocks and disappeared.

"Is it gone?" Michele gasped.

"I think so."

"I wish we were back in Chicago where there are no snakes," Michele said.

"Put your shoes on and let's get out of here," Michael said. "Wishing won't make it so."

"They're still muddy," Michele said.

"Muddy shoes are better than mad rattlesnakes," Michael said.

Michele grabbed her shoes. "Right," she said.

"We'll follow the stream for a while," Michael said. "At least we'll have fresh water to drink, and maybe we can find some berries or something to eat."

Miller dismounted at the water stop and carefully inspected the immediate ground around the tracks.

"Nothing," he said. "Everybody get down and check the area for tracks."

"They didn't get off here," Deeds said. "We didn't reach this water stop until two in the morning. They must have jumped off at the previous stop around eight."

Miller glanced at the sun.

"Two hours of daylight left," he said. "Not enough time to make the next water stop before dark. You boys make camp in that clearing over there. Frog, come with me. We'll keep looking for signs, just in case."

"What do we have left to eat?" Michael said.

"One chocolate bar, a few pieces of hard candy, and half the soda pop," Michele said.

"It's not much."

"It's all we have."

Michael nodded. "We can fill the pop bottle with water, but we need to find something else to eat besides candy."

"Like what?" Michele said. "We've been walking since last night and haven't seen one house or a person. Just that stupid snake, and I'm not eating him."

"Maybe there are fish in the stream," Michael said.

"And if there are, how do we catch them?" Michele said. "We don't have a fishing pole and bait. We haven't got a knife to scale them, and nothing to make a fire with to cook them if we did catch them."

"Maybe we have something in the satchel we could use?" Michael said.

"Like what?"

"I don't know," Michael said. "We'll check in the morning. Let's eat and find a place to sleep. It's getting dark."

Miller and Frog drank coffee from tin cups as they sat around a campfire. Deeds, Pep, Houle, and Ferris were already in their bedrolls for the night.

"Say we pick up their trail in the morning, do we bring them back to Medicine Bow and continue on with the plan as before?" Frog said.

"We'll pick them up," Miller said. "We lost too much time to head back to Medicine Bow. South of here is a ghost town called Silver Springs. Went dry about ten years ago. We'll keep the brats there and I'll go to Medicine Bow and send the wire to Chicago. Same plan, different location."

"You're sure she'll pay? I don't want to go through all this for nothing but a camping trip."

"She'll pay. The brats are all she has left as family heirs. She'll pay."

Frog sipped his coffee. "What if someone has picked up those kids?"

"They'll live to regret it," Miller said. "Come on, let's get some sleep. I want to be tracking by first light."

In soft grass at the base of a tree, Michael and Michele settled in for a night's sleep. The stream was less than a hundred feet away. The moon was up and bright, and it was much warmer than the previous night.

Frogs at the stream began to croak.

An owl hooted in the dark.

Crickets came to life and made a racket.

And then, way off in the distance, a wolf howled.

"Michael, what is that?" Michele whispered.

"I think it's a wolf," Michael said. "But I think it's far enough away that it won't bother us."

"Michael, I'm scared," Michele whispered and tucked her face into Michael's chest.

"I think we're okay here," Michael said. "Go to sleep."

Michele nodded and closed her eyes.

The wolf howled again.

And it sounded just a little bit closer.

# NINE

Frog inspected what was left of the footprints near the tracks at the second water stop east of Medicine Bow. The heavy rain didn't quite wash them all away,

"They got off here," he said and picked up a piece of a broken button.

Atop his horse Miller said, "Can you tell which direction they went?"

"Rain washed out their tracks from this point on," Frog said.

Miller dismounted. "They didn't go west toward Medicine Bow," he said. "I don't think they went east along the tracks. They probably headed for cover away from the railroad."

"How far you figure they could have gone on foot?" Frog said.

"No more than six or seven miles," Miller said. "Frog, you and Deeds come south with me. You other boys go north. Take what supplies you need. Whichever one of us finds them first, bring them back here and we'll join up later."

Frog grabbed the reins of his horse. "You heard the man, let's ride. We won't get rich standing around here gabbing."

"Mickey, I am so hungry," Michele said.

"I know. Me too," Michael said. "Let's see what we have left."

Michele opened the satchel and fished around inside for something to eat.

"We have two bites of the last chocolate bar, three pieces of hard candy, and the pop bottle full of water."

"Take one sip of water and save the rest for when it gets dark," Michael said.

Michele removed the cork, took a sip, and then passed the bottle to Michael. He took a smaller sip, replaced the cork, and set the bottle inside the satchel.

"Let's go," Michael said.

"We're almost out of daylight," Miller said as he watched Frog ascend a steep hill through binoculars.

"Those kids are a bigger pain than I thought they'd be," Deeds said.

"Hey, Frank!" Frog shouted from atop the hill. "Come have a look at this."

Miller and Deeds dismounted and left their horses tied to a bush as they ascended the hill. When they reached Frog, he pointed to the descending side of the hill.

"Something slid down this hill after the rain when it was muddy," Frog said. "See there past the grass?"

"It had to be them kids," Deeds said. "They got caught in that rain when this was all mud."

"Frog, see if you can pick up a trail down there," Miller said. "We'll bring the horses and follow you."

"Michael, it's almost dark," Michele said. "We have to stop."

"I know," Michael said. "Let's find a place to sleep."

"Wait," Michele said. "Do you smell something?"

"Like what?"

"I don't know. Something."

Michael sniffed the air several times and nodded. "I do smell something."

"It smells like . . . like . . . somebody's cooking," Michele said.

"Yeah."

"Maybe it's Indians?" Michele said.

"I don't think so," Michael said. "If there were Indians around here, we'd'a seen them by now."

"What should we do?"

"Follow our noses."

"They went to that creek over there to wash up, and it looks like they followed it downstream," Frog said.

"Be dark in about fifteen minutes," Miller said. "We could follow the creek for a while or make camp. My guess is they stayed close to fresh water, so it shouldn't be too hard to pick them up. What do you say, Frog, Deeds?"

"Might be easier to get a fresh start on rested horses in the morning," Frog said. "Them kids aren't going nowhere out here like this."

"I agree," Deeds said. "We can pick up their trail easy enough."

"Let's make camp and get a fire going," Miller said.

"Wait," Michael said. "I think it's coming from that way."

Michele sniffed the air. "I think you're right."

"It's dark now, so be careful," Michael said.

"Well, hold my hand then," Michele said.

Michael took hold of Michele's hand, and they turned from the stream and walked toward the open plains. The tall grass was wet with evening dew and dampened their shoes and pant legs.

They walked about a hundred yards and, as the sky darkened completely, Michael spotted a tiny red dot far away on the horizon.

"Do you see that?" he said.

"Yes."

"I think it's a fire," Michael said. "And I'll bet somebody is cooking on it."

"Maybe they'll give us some food?" Michele said.

"Or maybe they'll kill us."

"Why? Why would they kill us? Do you think it's Mr. Miller out there?"

"I don't know, but there's only one way to find out," Michael said. "Come on."

"Michael, if it's Mr. Miller we . . ."

"We won't get that close," Michael said. "Come on."

"I'm afraid."

"Me, too, but I'm starving."

"We won't get too close?"

"No."

"All right, but take my hand," Michele said.

Michael took his sister's hand and they slowly walked toward the glowing red dot and the smell of food cooking in a fry pan.

★ ★ ★ ★ ★

# The Cowboy

★ ★ ★ ★ ★

# TEN

The one thing that Matthew Quirk didn't count on when he set out on the drive east to Omaha was his cook and friend of ten years dropping dead in the middle of a seemingly normal conversation.

But that's exactly what happened.

On the ninth day out while having breakfast around the campfire, they were discussing which open range was the best available route to take based on water and grazing land. Old Johnson suddenly dropped his plate, looked at Quirk, and without another word he keeled over dead.

There wasn't a mark on Johnson's body, so Quirk figured his age finally caught up to the old cook and his heart just gave out. Died with his eyes wide open and a look of disbelief on his face.

Quirk had seen many die a lot worse.

That was three days ago and, after he put his old friend in the ground, things got even worse. It was impossible to drive the herd of two hundred fifty cattle and one hundred head of horses from the saddle and drive the chuck wagon at the same time. He had to leave the chuck wagon and drive the herd a few miles, then turn around and ride back for the wagon.

It was the only way he could drive the herd and still eat.

He made only nine miles in three days. Mostly because the herd was young and unbroken, and without Johnson to drive the wagon, Quirk couldn't ride point and steer the herd. When he rode back for the wagon, the young bulls dispersed the cows, and he had to waste time rounding them up again.

Then that lightning storm scattered the herd, and he spent an entire day rounding them up yet again and lost another full day of driving.

In any event, he would have to do something about his situation and soon.

At this rate he wouldn't reach Omaha until winter. The cattle would arrive skinny, and the horses would be useless for anything other than making glue out of. He would never get another beef and horse contract with the army if he arrived late, that was for sure. The army traveled on its stomach, and if he couldn't provide for that stomach, they would fill it elsewhere.

As he sipped his coffee, Quirk came to the realization he would have to leave the herd to ride to the nearest town and hire a new cook, or at least somebody to drive the chuck wagon and keep up.

That posed a whole new set of problems.

The round trip could take as long as six days. He could return with a new cook and find rustlers had made off with the herd and chuck wagon in his absence. Or the herd could take it upon itself and decide to scatter, and it would take another week to gather them up again.

His only option was to keep moving the herd and backtracking and hope to meet a stranger looking for work and hire him on to drive the wagon.

Quirk sipped his coffee and dug out his well-worn pipe. It belonged to his father a long time ago. He filled the bowl with tobacco from his pouch, stuck a twig into the campfire, and then used the twig to light the bowl.

It was a quiet night, cool and perfect for sleeping. The cattle and horses were calm, and the rising moon would be bright and full in a little while.

And then something disturbed the quiet. A few horses in the field snorted and then a few more made nervous whinnies, and that set the cattle on alert.

Cattle didn't go on alert without a good reason.

Quirk scanned the immediate area. Past the campfire it was too dark to see much, so he kept still and let his ears do the work.

The horses snorted nervously.

The cattle started to moo and kick about.

Whatever the reason for the disturbance, Quirk needed to check on it before the bulls took it upon themselves to stampede into the dark. That would scatter the herd for miles in every direction.

Quirk set the cup aside and stood up. His Winchester 73 rifle rested against his saddle, and he picked it up, cocked the lever to chamber a round, and then stood motionless to listen.

Seconds ticked off and then he heard it. The low rumbling growl of a wolf on the hunt somewhere in the distance.

Walking quickly, Michael held Michele's hand and almost dragged her along behind him.

"Michael, stop," Michele gasped. "I have to catch my breath."

"It's not that far now," Michael said. "Just over there."

"I know, but let me rest for just a minute."

Michael stopped and released Michele's hand.

"Okay, but just for a minute," Michael said.

"My side hurts," Michele said.

"That's from . . ." Michael said and paused.

After a few seconds Michele said, "From what?"

"Shhhh," Michael said. "Listen."

"I don't hear . . ."

The wolf growled softly in the darkness.

And he was close.

Michael grabbed Michele's hand.

"I think it's a wolf," he said. "We saw one once at the Chicago Zoo, remember?"

"What do we do?"

"Run!"

Quirk walked past the campfire and peered into the darkness. The wolf was close, and getting closer by the second, and its intention was a meal.

Spooked, the horses started to disperse.

And the faint outline of something came streaking past the horses.

Prey.

And whatever it was took a fall.

Seconds later, the snarling wolf emerged and jumped high into the air to pounce upon its prey.

Before the wolf landed on its helpless victim, Quirk fired one shot from the Winchester. With a loud yelp, the wolf fell from the air and hit the ground.

But it wasn't dead yet.

Quirk lowered the Winchester and sighed.

He disliked killing an animal unnecessarily, but having seen the herd, the wolf would return, bringing others, and the pack would start killing the stock.

Quirk walked about seventy-five feet to the fallen wolf. It was mortally wounded but still alive. He slowly withdrew his Colt Peacemaker from the holster and cocked it.

"I'm sorry to kill you, but I can't have you picking off my stock," Quirk said and shot the wolf a second time, finishing the job.

Frog opened his eyes and looked over at Miller.

"You hear that?" Frog said. "Two shots."

"I heard," Miller said.

"Somebody shooting at somebody in the dark, you think?" Frog said.

"I think somebody took down that wolf we heard growling in the dark not long ago," Miller said. "First shot was a rifle. The second was a pistol to finish it off. From the echo of the report of the rounds, I'd put him at a distance of about three miles or so from us. No more than that."

"Maybe whoever that is has seen those kids," Frog said.

"I'm sure we'll run into him in the morning," Miller said. "I'll be sure to ask him just that."

They ran as fast as they could, but the wolf closed the gap and ran them down. After all, he had four legs to their two. When it was no use anymore, Michael threw Michele to the ground and covered her body with his. Maybe the wolf would be content just to eat him and, with a full belly, leave Michele alone.

Michael heard the wolf jump, and he braced himself for the attack, but a gunshot sounded and the wolf yelped and fell to the ground behind them.

Michael turned his head and watched from the darkness as a man walked to the wolf, pulled out his six-gun, shot it a second time, and killed it.

Then the man walked away and disappeared into the shadows.

"Michael," Michele whispered.

"Quiet," Michael whispered. "Don't make a sound."

"I can't breathe," Michele whispered.

As quietly as possible, Michael rolled off his sister and looked at her.

"Are you hurt?" Michael whispered.

"I don't think so," Michele whispered. "Are you?"

"No. Come on," Michael whispered and extended his hand.

★ ★ ★ ★ ★

There we no signs of the wolf's prey, so Quirk checked the horses and stock. A few horses ran downfield, but most stayed put. Same with the cattle. They sensed the wolf was dead and no longer a threat to them. Come morning, he would check for strays and round them up before moving the herd.

He returned to the fire and built it up high enough to last until morning. If any more wolves or coyotes were about, they would think twice about approaching so large a flame. Especially after hearing two gunshots. Most wolves and coyotes that lived long enough learned that man and his guns meant danger and death, and they knew to stay away from anything on two legs.

Taking a seat against his saddle, Quirk relit the pipe. Beyond the fire the night had grown still again. Even the horses and stock had quieted down. Whatever was running from the wolf was long gone and would surely not return.

After a time, Quirk extinguished the pipe and crawled into his bedroll.

Just to be on the safe side of things, he kept the Winchester close by his side.

"Is it dead?" Michele whispered.

On his hands and knees Michael looked at the dead wolf.

"Yes," he whispered. "It's dead."

"What about that man?" Michele whispered.

"I think he's a cowboy from the looks of him, and I think he went to sleep," Michael whispered.

"What do we do now?" Michele whispered.

"Come with me," Michael whispered.

Michael led Michele to the covered chuck wagon.

"Keep watch for me," Michael whispered. "I'm going to find us something to eat in here."

"Michael, don't," Michele whispered.

"Just keep watch," Michael said and as quietly as possible, he climbed up the rear of the chuck wagon and into it.

"Michael!" Michele whispered in a panic.

"Be quiet," Michael whispered from inside the chuck wagon.

Michele kept watch for the cowboy for what seemed like the longest time until finally Michael stuck his head up.

"Take this," he said and handed her a giant can of peaches. "And this," he said and handed her sticks of beef jerky.

Carefully, Michael climbed down from the chuck wagon and took the can of peaches from Michele.

"Let's go," he whispered.

"Wait. Our satchel," Michele whispered.

"I'll get it. You go find a spot to sit over there someplace."

Holding the jerky, Michele walked about two hundred feet away from the chuck wagon and sat down beside a tree. A few moments later Michael showed up with the satchel and can of peaches.

He sat beside her.

"Must be two pounds of peaches in this can," he said.

"And how do we open that can of two pounds of peaches, Mr. Smarty-pants?"

Michael looked at the sealed metal can.

"Damn," he said.

"Aunt Angela would wash your mouth out with soap for using that word," Michele said.

"Aunt Angela isn't here with a can opener," Michael said. "And it's her fault we're in this mess anyway."

"Let's eat the jerky," Michele said. "We can find—"

"Be right back," Michael said and dashed off.

"Michael, you come back here," Michele said, but he was gone.

While she waited for Michael to return, Michele ate a full stick of jerky. It was sweet and chewy and delicious. She was going to eat another when Michael returned.

"I got this," he said and showed her the can opener. "And this," he said and showed her the large chocolate bar and full bottle of soda pop.

"What if he catches us?" Michele said.

"He's asleep. I heard him snoring like a buzz saw at a mill."

"Let's eat the jerky and save the peaches and chocolate for tomorrow morning," Michele said.

"Good idea," Michael said. "Then let's find a place to sleep down by the stream so we'll have fresh water."

A hundred yards away from the glowing campfire, Michael and Michele found a soft spot of grass near the stream to sleep on for the night.

"Michael, are you asleep yet?" Michele said.

"No."

"I was thinking about that wolf," Michele said.

"What about it?"

"He would have killed us."

"That's for sure."

"When you thought he caught us, you threw me on the ground and covered me," Michele said. "To protect me from the wolf."

"I tripped."

"No you didn't, you liar," Michele said. "You pretend all the time like you don't love me but you do."

Michael sighed.

"And we both know it," Michele said.

"Okay, so what? Go to sleep."

"So quit pretending like you hate me all the time, because nobody believes it anyway."

"Why don't you pretend that you're going to sleep?"

"I'm too cold to sleep," Michele said.

Michael extended his arm and Michael fell into his embrace. "Goodnight, Mickey," she said.

# ELEVEN

While the coffee percolated and the beans and bacon cooked in the fry pan, Quirk took quick stock of the herd.

Maybe a dozen horses had wandered off and the like amount in cattle. It wouldn't take more than two hours to round them up, and he could maybe make five or six miles before turning back for the chuck wagon.

He ate breakfast, saddled his horse, and rode off to find the stray horses and cattle.

"Is he gone?" Michele said from behind a tree.

"Yes. Be right back," Michael said. "I have to find us some more food."

"This is stealing," Michele said. "Stealing is wrong."

"Do you want to starve to death before we find a house or town and be right, or eat and find a way out of this mess?"

"Okay, but be careful."

"Keep watch."

"All right, but hurry."

Michael ran to the chuck wagon and climbed in through the back. There were wood barrels of bacon wrapped in salt paper, coffee, beans, flour, cornmeal, jerked beef, and a wood crate with six bottles of whiskey, a dozen large cans of fruit, and a case of canned milk. There were pots, pans, coffee pots, and cutlery and a bunch of other interesting things Michael didn't have time to look at. He grabbed some sticks of jerky, a can of condensed milk and a can of pears, two forks and a spoon and jumped out of the wagon and ran back to Michele.

"Let's eat and then get going," Michael said. "I don't want to get caught by that cowboy. No telling what he'll do. He looked pretty mean when he shot that wolf."

They ate some peaches from last night's can and two sticks of jerky. Michael used the can opener to make an opening in the can of milk. It came out like thick syrup.

"It's condensed milk," Michele said.

"I know," Michael said. "Pour some on the spoon and lick it. It's sweet."

They each drank two spoonfuls of milk, and then Michael packed everything away in the satchel.

"Which way should we go?" Michele said.

"Let's keep along the stream," Michael said. "We're bound to find a house sooner or later. People need water, right?"

"Maybe we should ask the cowboy for help," Michele suggested. "Maybe he's not as mean as we think."

"I don't think—"

The pounding of horse hooves silenced Michael.

They peered around the tree. The cowboy returned with the stray horses. He dismounted at the chuck wagon and loaded up various items from his camp. Then he selected two horses from the pack, led them to the chuck wagon, and secured them with long reins so they could wander and eat grass, but not escape.

He patted each horse and gave them sugar cubes.

Then he mounted his horse, removed a thin whip from the saddle, rode in an arc around the horses, and cracked the whip a few times. The horses followed him and, to the amazement of the twins, so did the cattle.

"He's leaving the wagon full of food," Michele said.

"Lucky us," Michael said.

★ ★ ★ ★ ★

Quirk drove the herd hard for about three miles. He normally wouldn't drive them so hard, but they would have plenty of time to rest while he rode back for the chuck wagon.

He dismounted and gave his horse a short break. He smoked his pipe while he watched the cattle and horses pick out their spots to eat tall sweet grass on the open range.

Then Quirk mounted up and rode back to the chuck wagon.

Michael and Michael stood in the rear of the chuck wagon and peered inside.

"Why do you suppose he left all this food?" Michael said.

"I don't think he left it," Michele said. "I think he's coming back for it."

"How do you know?"

"Because there he is."

Michael looked around the wagon. The cowboy was riding directly toward the wagon at full steam.

"Hide," Michael said.

"He'll see us."

"Not if we hide," Michael said. "Get in the wagon."

"What?"

"Get in the wagon."

"I don't—"

Michael grabbed Michele by the legs, lifted her over the floor of the wagon, and tossed her inside.

Then he climbed over and joined her.

"Michael, we can't—"

"Hide under those blankets behind the barrels," Michael said. "He won't see us if he looks inside."

Quirk dismounted at the chuck wagon and tied his horse to the right side of the buckboard. Then he hitched the two horses he'd left behind to the wagon and climbed onto the seat.

With a crack of the reins, the horses moved the wagon forward.

The ride to the herd was slow going and took more than an hour to cover the three miles.

As he neared the herd, Quirk spotted trouble. Three men on horseback were riding, cautiously and slowly, into the herd, looking about for something.

Quirk pulled the double-barreled shotgun he kept under the seat, cocked both hammers, and then rode slowly to meet the men.

The three men spotted the approaching wagon, turned their horses, and slowly rode to meet it.

Quirk stopped the wagon and aimed the shotgun in their direction.

"That's far enough to suit me," Quirk said.

"We mean you no harm, friend," Miller said. "We were just riding by."

"Maybe so, but that's my herd you're poking around in, and it's small enough as it is," Quirk said.

"My name is Frank Miller," Miller said. He moved his vest out of the way to show his Illinois Detective Agency badge. "I operate the Illinois Detective Agency and these are my associates, Mr. Tiller and Mr. Deeds."

"You're a long way from home, Mr. Miller," Quirk said.

"We were hired to transport two children from Chicago to San Francisco," Miller said. "They jumped the train at a water stop near Medicine Bow. We're trying to find them before something happens to them."

"Two children?" Quirk said.

"A boy and girl, twins," Miller said. "Twelve years old. We followed them to the creek over there and lost them last night in the dark."

"Twins?" Quirk said. "They jumped the train, you say?"

Miller nodded. "A boy and a girl, like I said."

"I've been driving my herd for ten days and haven't seen a soul besides you," Quirk said.

"How come you driving your own wagon?" Frog said.

"My man died a few days ago," Quirk said. "I buried him about twenty miles back. I'm hoping to hire on a new man if I can find one."

"Maybe we should take a look in that wagon," Frog said.

Quirk turned the shotgun on Frog. "And maybe if you just stay on your horse, you'll live longer than if you go poking your nose where it don't belong," he said.

"We mean you know harm, mister," Miller said. "We're just trying to find those children before something happens to them, is all."

"You won't find them in my wagon," Quirk said. "They probably stayed close to the creek for fresh water. Why did they run away anyway?"

"Parents died," Miller said. "Their aunt in Chicago was sending them to live with family in San Francisco. I guess they didn't want to go and lit out on their own in the dark at a water stop."

"If I see them, I'll hold them for you," Quirk said.

"I'm afraid I'm going to have to check your wagon," Miller said.

"I told you I haven't seen them," Quirk said.

"Isn't it possible that when you left the wagon unattended, they might have come across it without you knowing it?" Miller said. "Isn't it possible they could have snuck on board while you weren't around to see them?"

Quirk slowly nodded his head. "Yeah, it's possible," he admitted.

"Mr. Tiller, check the wagon," Miller said.

Frog slowly rode to the rear of the chuck wagon and peered

inside. He carefully looked at the barrels and crates, pots and pans, stacked blankets and such, and then rode back to Miller and Deeds.

"Just supplies," Frog said.

"I told you that," Quirk said.

"We'd be derelict in our duty if we didn't check," Miller said. "So no hard feelings."

"I can't hold it against a man for doing his job. Good luck finding them kids before something happens to them," Quirk said.

"Say, last night did you do some shooting?" Frog said.

"Wolf," Quirk said. "Went for the herd about three miles back. I had to put him down or he'd call out his entire pack."

Miller nodded. "Come on, boys," he said.

Quirk waited for them to be out of sight before he de-cocked the shotgun and set it back under the seat. Then he locked the brake and stepped down.

"I hate to leave you here," Quirk told the team mounted to the chuck wagon. "But I have to make another six or seven miles before nightfall."

"He's gone, Michael," Michele said. "You can get off of me now."

Michael lifted the wool blanket off his head and peered out the back of the wagon. Then he stood and gave Michele a hand standing up.

"That was close," Michael said. "Too close."

"Do you think they'll come back?" Michele said.

"I don't know," Michael said. "Maybe."

"What are we going to do?" Michele said. "We're trapped out here."

"Not if we travel at night when they're all sleeping," Michael said.

"Yeah," Michele said. "But what do we do in the meantime?"

"Wait."

"Where?"

"Right here in this chuck wagon," Michael said. "Unless you got a better place to hide?"

Quirk brushed his horse while he waited for the coffee to boil in the pot. He made eleven miles today, not nearly enough, but a bit more than he expected under the present set of circumstances.

When the coffee was ready, he filled a cup and started a supper of bacon, beans, and jerked beef. If he had room afterward, he'd open a can of peaches as a treat.

The sky was near dusk when he spotted Miller and his two men riding toward him. They were riding hard to beat the quickly approaching night.

Quirk lit his pipe, settled in against his saddle with his back to them, and waited for them to arrive.

When they finally reached his camp, Quirk didn't bother to turn around.

"Hey, cowboy, it's Frank Miller," Miller said.

"I know who it is," Quirk said.

"Can we camp here for the night?" Miller said.

"Come ahead," Quirk said. "I'll throw some extra food on the fire."

Fortunately for the twins, Quirk didn't look behind the large barrel filled with flour where they hid under wool blankets. He took what he needed from the slab of salted bacon and beans and coffee and never glanced their way.

"What do we do now, Mr. Smarty-pants?" Michele whispered.

"We wait for them to go to sleep," Michael whispered. "Then

we sneak out and find a place to hide until morning."

"I'm sorry we can't help you drive your wagon in the morning, but we need to make time if we're going to find those kids," Miller said.

"Another two days' ride west and a day's ride south is Summerville," Quirk said. "I should be able to find a driver for the wagon there. With some luck, I'll make Omaha inside a month."

"Why Omaha?" Miller asked.

"Army contract for beef and trained horses," Quirk said. "I have two commitments a year."

"That doesn't leave you time for much else," Miller said.

Quirk grinned. "It surely doesn't."

"You're a fair hand with a fry pan, I admit," Frog said.

"I do most of my own cooking on the ranch," Quirk said. "My old-timer hired on for the drives. It gave him something else to do besides sit on the porch, chew tobacco, and drink whiskey all day."

"He just up and died, you say?" Frog said.

"He was seventy-two with a lot of bad habits," Quirk said. "I guess his old heart was just worn out."

"Before you said Summerville," Miller said. "Silver Springs is closer by a day."

"Ghost town since 'seventy-seven," Quirk said. "People moved south to work on the railroad and never went back. Built a whole new railroad town I heard, but I never had cause to visit."

"Sorry to hear that," Miller said. "I rode through there in 'seventy-five once. Seemed like a nice budding town."

"It was," Quirk said. "Well, I'm going to turn in. I got nothing but long days ahead of me."

★ ★ ★ ★ ★

With the satchel loaded full of cans of fruit and jerky, Michael and Michele quietly climbed out of the wagon and made their way down to the stream. They found a place in the dark well out of view of Quirk and Miller and the others.

"What do we do now, Michael?" Michele asked.

"Eat."

"I mean tomorrow and the next day. We just can't keep hiding in his wagon like this. He's going to notice all the food we've taken or catch us red-handed. Then what?"

"You heard him say he was going to that town called Summerville," Michael said. "We can hide out that long and go there and find some help. A policeman or marshal. They have to help us. It's their job to help people."

"That's not a bad idea," Michele said. "When we tell them what happened, they'll have to send us to San Francisco and arrest Mr. Miller for what he did."

"Let's eat and get some sleep," Michael said. "We have to get up before they do."

"Open that can of pears," Michele said. "I like those."

# Twelve

"Well," Miller said, and extended his right hand to Quirk. "Maybe we'll cross paths again. Good luck, cowboy."

Quirk shook Miller's hand. "You too, with finding those kids," Quirk said. "If I run across them, I'll bring them to Summerville and send word to you by general telegram."

"Appreciate that," Miller said. "I'll give you a reward if you do come across them." He looked at Frog and Deeds. "Let's ride. There's another storm dogging us, and we don't want to ride into it."

Quirk looked at the sky. The dark clouds forming on the horizon meant trouble. He had about six hours to move the herd before the storm arrived and put an end to the day's travel.

Quirk extinguished the campfire, rinsed off the fry pans and coffee pot, saddled his horse, and drove the herd east.

Michael came out of hiding first to make sure everybody had gone, and then he signaled to Michele. Together they walked to the wagon.

"Did you hear what he said about a storm coming?" Michele said.

Michael nodded. "Look at the sky."

"Michael, Mr. Quirk seems like a nice man," Michele said. "Maybe we should ask him to help us?"

"You heard what Mr. Miller said," Michael said. "He'd give a reward for turning us in. No, we have to hide until we reach that town. Then we'll go to the police like we planned."

"Okay, Michael," Michele said. "We'll go to the police."

"Come on, let's eat some breakfast," Michael said and climbed into the wagon.

Quirk pushed the herd harder than he had the last few days. He wanted to drive as many miles as possible before the storm hit and scattered them to the winds. After about seven miles, Quirk left the herd in an open range, gave his horse a thirty-minute rest, and then made the return trip.

He reached the chuck wagon an hour before the storm hit, hitched up the team, and, with his horse in tow, drove the wagon as fast as the team could pull it.

The herd was scattered about the range as the darkening clouds and sizzle of electricity in the air made them ill at ease. They sensed the storm, and lightning and thunder frightened them, even the bulls.

Quirk parked the wagon in the center of the herd to show them he was around. Then he set the team free and hobbled his horse to the side of the wagon so he wouldn't get spooked and run off with the others. He removed the saddle and stuck it under the wagon to keep it from getting soaked or trampled upon.

Then the early afternoon sky grew as dark as midnight, and the horses and cattle nervously grunted and milled about the range.

When that first flash of lightning lit up the sky, the herd was thrown into a panic. A few seconds after the flash of lightning, a hard, booming thunderclap sounded, and the rain started to fall.

"Well, we're in for it now," Quirk told his horse and then crawled into the back of the chuck wagon.

The rain seemed to come down in sheets of water. At one

point Quirk heard lightning strike a nearby tree and the tree split and crash to the ground. Thunder seemed to boom every few seconds. The ground outside the wagon flooded from the torrential downpour.

The storm was the kind of summer storm that blew in quickly, hit hard, and moved on just as quickly. Quirk had been caught in many such a storm. Then the rain eased up a bit and the sky outside the wagon slowly grew lighter.

The worst of it was over.

When the rain finally stopped altogether, Quirk stepped out of the wagon and into ankle-deep mud.

He looked at the rear wheels on the wagon. They were a foot deep in mud, and he knew the wagon wasn't going anywhere without him digging them out by hand. His horse, tethered to the wagon, was wet and standing in the mud but seemed no worse for wear. He dug a few sugar cubes out of his shirt pocket and held his hand out to his horse. The horse gobbled them up in one lick. With a blanket from the wagon, he wiped the water off his horse so he could air-dry.

Then Quirk stepped out of the mud and surveyed the herd. More than half of the cattle had scattered as had most of the horses. It would take an entire day or more to gather them all up again, never mind the hours required to free up the wagon from the mud it was stuck in.

The day was wasted anyway, so he might as well tackle the wagon first. Quirk removed his shirt and undershirt and then dug out the shovel from inside the wagon.

The mud was heavy. Each shovelful weighed thirty or more pounds. By the time he had cleared the rear wheels, his bare chest and arms and most of his pants were covered in mud.

Quirk got behind the wagon and pushed as hard as he could, but only managed to rock the wagon slightly and not free it.

"All right, boy, it's your turn," Quirk said to his horse.

Quirk walked his horse to the hitching post in front of the wagon and secured him tightly. Taking the reins in his hand, Quirk walked the horse forward.

The chuck wagon rocked in the mud.

"You got to do better than that," Quirk said and tugged on the reins.

Using his powerful front legs, Quirk's horse pulled. The chuck wagon rocked and finally broke free of the very deep mud.

"Good boy," Quirk said and patted the horse's neck.

Quirk unhitched his horse and allowed him to freely roam the nearby open range with some of the other horses that hadn't run off during the storm.

"Well, I guess I'm next," Quirk said.

He dug a bar of soap out of the wagon and walked the fifty yards to the stream where he removed his gun belt and boots.

Holding the bar of soap, Quirk walked into the stream to the center where it was waist-deep and then dove under.

"Damn, that's cold," Quirk said when he resurfaced.

Quirk sat in front of a roaring campfire and allowed the heat to dry the pants and socks he had hung across a line of rope tied to two sticks. The long underwear he always wore under his pants were a mess, not worth saving. He dug a clean pair out of the wagon, removed the old pair, and put on the clean. Then he tossed the old pair into the fire and added a few more sticks of wood to it.

Quirk filled his pipe with tobacco, lit it off a stick that he set in the fire, and then smoked quietly for a few minutes as he watched the sky glow orange and yellow from the slowly setting sun.

This was Quirk's favorite time of the day, the sunset. The sky reminded him of some paintings he saw once in a museum in Denver a few years back. The yellow and red colors seemed to glow in the light and jump off the canvas right at you. He couldn't remember the name of the artist, just that the name began with the letter R, but the sky at this time of day always reminded him of those paintings.

When his pants and socks were finally dry, Quirk dressed and put on his heavy boots and finally his gun belt.

There was nothing much left to do for the day except fix some supper. He entered the wagon for the pans, coffee pot, bacon, beans, and some jerky. He noticed supplies were getting a bit low and made a mental list of things to buy in Summerville.

He missed the old man's small sour biscuits and flapjacks he prepared in the morning and the hearty biscuits for the evening meal. On cold evenings, the old man would add an ounce of bourbon whiskey to the bacon and beans for flavoring and to ward off the chill of the night air. Quirk dug out the whiskey bottle and added an ounce or two to the fry pan, then lifted the bottle to toast the old man and took a swallow.

Quirk ate his fill and then smoked another bowl on his pipe while he drank his coffee. By then the stars were just showing themselves in the dark sky, and he figured to turn in early and be up well before dawn.

If he were to make up for lost time, he would have to ride sunup to sundown for the next several weeks, and even then it would be cutting things close to the edge. He fixed the bedroll close to the fire, added some extra wood, and settled in for some much-needed sleep.

Still damp from the heavy rain, Michael and Michele stayed in their hiding place inside a clump of bushes. They were chilled from their damp clothes and the colder night air after the sun went down.

"Michael, I'm freezing," Michele said with chattering teeth.

"Me, too," Michael said. "Maybe I could build a fire?"

"He'll see that."

"He's asleep."

"Then he'd smell it and wake up, and we'd be in a real fix."

"I have an idea," Michael said. "Wait here."

As Michael crawled out of the brush, Michele said, "Mickey, don't leave me."

"I'll be right back," Michael said. "Don't worry."

"Mickey, wait," Michele said, but Michael had already taken off walking.

Michael walked in the dark toward the chuck wagon, using the last bit of light from the dying campfire as a guide.

When he reached the rear of the wagon Michael quietly climbed into it, selected two wool blankets from the pile, and then snuck back out with them. Walking quickly, he returned to the brush and crawled inside to Michele.

"I got these," Michael said and showed Michele the blankets.

"I don't feel so well, Michael," Michele said.

"Wrap a blanket around you and get warm," Michael said.

Michael helped Michele to sit up, and then he draped the blanket around her body. Then he got down next to her and tossed the second blanket over the both of them.

"You should warm up now," Michael said.

"Thank you, Mickey," Michele said and hugged her brother.

"Try to get some sleep," Michael said. "You'll feel better."

Michele kissed him on the cheek and he wrapped his arm around her.

"Now go to sleep," Michael said. "You'll feel better in the morning."

Hours before dawn, Michael woke up when Michele moaned in her sleep. The blankets were soaking wet with sweat. Michele was drenched. At first he thought she'd made water in her sleep.

But when he touched her face, she was burning up with fever.

"Mikey, wake up," Michael whispered.

Even in the dark, Michael could see her teeth chattering. When he touched her arm, she was shivering. Drenched in sweat and shivering with cold. She was awful sick, he reasoned, to sweat and shiver like this.

Unsure what to do, Michael removed the blankets, dug out the bottle of water, and poured some on his pocket handkerchief. He dabbed the wet handkerchief on her face and neck.

Michele moaned in her sleep at his touch. Then she started talking in her sleep, crying about their parents and San Francisco.

For the next hour or so, Michael dabbed cool water on Michele's face. Then he heard a noise and poked his head out of the brush. The sky was lightening just a bit.

The cowboy was awake and building a campfire.

"Michele, wake up," Michael said and shook her.

Michele moaned softly in her sleep. Her skin was even hotter than before. He was afraid she was going to die.

He didn't know what else to do so Michael crawled out of the brush and walked toward the cowboy.

Quirk was drinking a hot cup of coffee and watching the morning sky start to brighten the sky when his horse nervously whinnied behind him. He took another sip and set the cup on the buckboard of the chuck wagon to his left.

Then in one smooth motion, Quirk grabbed his Peacemaker from its holster and spun around, cocking it at the same time.

"Whoever you are, I can drill you, so don't move and I won't have to," Quirk said.

There was a moment of quiet, and then Michael said from the dark, "Please, mister, I need your help. My sister is very sick."

"Come into the light by the fire so I can see you," Quirk said.

Michael walked forward until Quirk could see him.

"Why, you're just a kid," Quirk said and holstered the Peacemaker.

"My sister is . . ." Michael said.

"Are you trying to get yourself killed, sneaking up on a man in the dark of the morning like that?"

"No, but my sister—"

"You're the runaway Miller and his men are after?" Quirk said. "Ain't you?"

"Yes, sir," Michael said. "My sister is awful sick with a fever."

"A fever?"

"Burning up and freezing at the same time."

"Where?"

"I'll take you to her."

"Go on then."

Quirk followed Michael to the thick brush near the stream.

"In there?" Quirk said.

"Yes, sir."

Quirk knelt down and saw Michele's shoes and pants. He grabbed her ankles and carefully slid her out from the brush, careful not to scratch her on the thorns.

"You're right. This girl is burning up with fever," Quirk said when he touched her cheek. "For how long?"

"We got wet last night in the rain, and I think she caught a chill or something," Michael said.

Quirk looked at Michael. "Or something?" he said.

"Can you help her?" Michael said. "She's my sister. If something happens to her—"

"Quit sniveling like a baby and do as I say," Quirk snapped.

"Yes, sir," Michael said.

"Take her shoes, pants, and shirt off," Quirk said.

"She's a girl," Michael said.

"I know she's a girl," Quirk said. "Right now she's an alive girl, and if want to keep her that way, you'll do as I say and be right quick about it."

"Yes, sir."

"Quit calling me 'sir' and get her clothes off," Quirk said. "You can leave her undergarments on. Now hurry up, and I'll be right back."

Quirk ran back to the chuck wagon, tossed more wood onto the campfire, and then stripped down to his long underwear.

When he returned to Michael, he had removed Michele's clothing down to her camisole and pantaloons.

Quirk lifted Michele in his arms. She barely weighed eighty-five pounds, if that. He carried her to the stream, walked into the deepest part, and held her in his arms so that just her face was above water.

The water was cold; really, really cold.

Michele moaned in her sleep, but didn't open her eyes.

Quirk looked at Michael on shore.

"What are you looking at, boy?" Quirk said. "Go over to my camp, gather up some wood, and feed the fire. We have to keep it hot."

"Yes, sir," Michael said.

"Quit calling me . . . just go," Quirk said. "And return my blankets to camp and spread them out near the fire."

Quirk kept Michele in the water for fifteen minutes, then held her out for a minute or two and submerged her again for another fifteen. He did this over a period of two hours. The entire time Michael stayed close by on shore, except when he went to feed the fire. Every once in a while, Michael could see his sister shiver in the water and her lips turned blue.

"Is my coffee pot still in the fire?" Quirk said.

"Yes, sir."

"Fetch me a cup so I can warm up a bit."

Michael ran to the fire, filled a cup with hot coffee, and carried it back to Quirk. Holding Michele above water, Quirk reached for the cup and took a sip.

"My teeth were banging together like a Navajo war drum," Quirk said. "Thanks, boy."

Quirk finished the coffee and tossed the cup to Michael.

"Shouldn't be much longer," Quirk said.

When Quirk finally carried Michele to shore, her lips were still blue, but her fever had come down. Not all the way, but enough so that he thought she was out of immediate danger and wouldn't die.

He carried Michele to camp and gently lowered her onto the blankets.

"Cover her with one blanket," Quirk said. "I'll be right back."

Quirk grabbed a water bucket from the wagon, took it to the stream to fill it, and then returned to his camp. From the wagon Quirk removed several clean neckerchiefs and tossed them into the water bucket.

"Put one of those on her forehead," Quirk said. "Switch them out every few minutes so her face stays cold."

"Yes, sir," Michael said.

While Michael placed a wet neckerchief to Michele's forehead, Quirk went into the chuck wagon and returned with a pint bottle of bourbon whiskey and a spoon.

"Hold her head up for me so I get some of this in her," Quirk said.

"That's whiskey, sir," Michael said.

"I know what it is. It's mine, ain't it?" Quirk said. "Now do what I said and hold up her head."

Michael took hold of Michele and gently lifted her head. Quirk poured a small amount of bourbon onto the spoon, slowly dribbled the whiskey into Michele's mouth, and then held her nose closed.

Unable to breathe, she swallowed and coughed, but her eyes stayed closed.

"A little more, and then we'll let her rest," Quirk said.

After a second dose of bourbon, Michele coughed and gasped again and then settled down on the blankets and grew quiet and still.

"Grab her clothes and hang them by the fire to dry," Quirk said. "I'll fix us some breakfast."

"Yes, sir."

"And quit calling me 'sir,' " Quirk snapped.

"Why did you run away from the train?" Quirk said.

Michael spooned some beans into his mouth and washed them down with a sip of water from a tin cup.

"We had to, Mr. Quirk," Michael said. "Mr. Miller and his men were going to kidnap us off the train."

"Kidnap you?" Quirk said. "What for?"

"Our Aunt Angela in Chicago is very rich," Michael said. "Me and Mikey, I mean my sister, Michele, was going to live with relatives in San Francisco. Our parents died six months ago, and our aunt is unmarried and doesn't have time to raise us. She owns Dunn Investments and Steel Corporation. Mr. Miller was supposed to take us on the train to San Francisco, but I heard him planning to kidnap us and ask for seven hundred and fifty thousand dollars for each of us."

"Seven hundred and . . . Your aunt has that kind of money?" Quirk said.

"She is what they call a millionaire. She has a lot more than that."

"Then why doesn't she keep you herself?"

"She's not married, like I said, and doesn't have the time," Michael said. "She said we'd be better off being raised in a family that has a father."

"Spinster woman your aunt?"

"What's that, sir?" Michael asked.

"A woman who never married."

"I guess so, sir."

"Is she ugly?"

"No, sir. My aunt is actually very pretty."

"So what were you planning to do by running away?"

"Find a farmhouse and ask for help from the police or a marshal."

"Good plan, except you're in the middle of nowhere," Quirk said. "This is a cattle trail on the prairie. You could walk for weeks on end and not see a living soul. It's a small miracle wolves didn't get you before now."

"One almost did the other night," Michael said. "You shot it just before it attacked us."

"So that's what it was chasing," Quirk said.

"Sir, will—" Michael said.

"Call me 'sir' one more time, and I'll take a switch to you," Quirk said. "My name is Quirk. Matthew Quirk. Call me Matthew, or call me Mr. Quirk, I don't care which. Anything but sir."

"Yes . . . I mean, Mr. Quirk," Michael said. "Can you take us to a town so we can talk to the police or the marshal?"

"There are but a handful of small towns along the way to Omaha," Quirk said. "And most of them would be lucky to have a sheriff. There isn't a marshal within three hundred miles of here. Nearest one would be in Casper, and that's a far piece to the north."

"What are we supposed to do, sir? I mean Mr. Quirk."

"I'll tell you what I'm going to do, and that's round up my strays," Quirk said. "You stay with your sister until she wakes up. I'll study on the situation while I'm gone. Keep that fire going and the food hot. Your sister will be as hungry as a bear when she wakes up."

"What if someone comes along?"

"I've been on the trail three weeks now, and the only people I ran across are looking for you and they went east," Quirk said.

Quirk was gone close to an hour when Michele moaned softly a few times and then slowly opened her eyes. For a moment her vision was fuzzy and out of focus, but then it cleared and she looked up at Michael.

"Mickey?" she said.

"I'm right here," Michael said.

"What happened? Where am I?" Michele said.

"You had a fever," Michael said. "I got Mr. Quirk to help you. He's off looking for his stray cattle and horses."

"A fever?" Michele said. "Who took my clothes off?"

"I did so Mr. Quirk could dunk you in the creek to bring your fever down."

"Mr. Quirk saw me without clothes?" Michele said. "Michael, I'm a girl. How could you let him see me with my clothes off? That's not proper behavior and you very well know it."

"He couldn't very well dunk you in the creek with your clothes on, could he?" Michael said. "And they're dry now if you want to get dressed, Miss Proper."

"I'm hungry," Michele said.

"I figured that," Michael said. "There is bacon, beans, and condensed milk with water in it. You can have as much as you want Mr. Quirk said."

Michele sat up while Michael loaded a tin plate with hot food.

Michael tossed some dry wood onto the fire while Michele ate. "Mr. Quirk said we're in the middle of nowhere and there are no police for hundreds of miles," he said. "Someplace called Casper is the closest. I think that's in Wyoming."

"Where are my clothes?" Michele said when the plate was empty.

"I'll get them."

Michael removed the shirt and pants from the rope strung between two sticks behind the fire and gave them to Michele.

"Well," Michele said.

"Well what?"

"Turn around so I can get dressed."

Michael rolled his eyes. "I've already seen all there is to see and it wasn't that great to look at."

"Michael!" Michele snapped.

Michael turned his back and Michele dressed quickly. As she was putting on her shoes a gunshot sounded in the distance. It echoed and faded away.

"Maybe Mr. Quirk shot another wolf?" Michael said.

Michele stood beside Michael. "Yeah," she said.

It was late afternoon when Quirk returned to camp with his herd mostly intact. He guided them to the open range and then rode to the chuck wagon. The twins were standing beside the fire.

Quirk dismounted and removed two chickens from the saddle horn.

"Got us some prairie chickens for supper," Quirk said. "Girl, you pluck them. Boy, you tend to my horse. I have to make a count of the herd before dark."

Michele and Michael looked at Quirk.

"What's the matter, didn't you hear me?" Quirk said.

"I don't know what 'pluck' means," Michele said.

"And I don't know how to tend a horse," Michael said.

"That's right, you're city kids," Quirk said. "Well, can you count?"

"Of course," Michele said. "We're highly educated you know.

We can do math problems in out head and even speak some Latin words."

"Not so educated you can feed yourselves without stealing," Quirk said. "Okay, boy you go count the cows. Girl, you count the horses. Be careful not to get too close to the bulls. Some of them are a bit testy around small children, especially the educated ones."

When Michael and Michele returned to the chuck wagon Quirk was cutting up the chickens on the cutting block that folded out from the side of the wagon. He used a large meat cleaver to cut through the bones.

"Two hundred and forty-seven cows, Mr. Quirk," Michael said.

"And I counted ninety-six horses," Michele said.

Quirk nodded. "Them strays could be miles from here by now. Well, I'll just have to let them be this time. I can't waste another day on such a small count of missing stock."

"Mr. Quirk, we . . ." Michael said.

"Hold on a minute," Quirk said. "Girl, go in the wagon and fetch the big fry pan, a cup of flour, the salt and pepper. Boy, load up the campfire with wood."

Michele climbed into the wagon to get the items Quirk asked for. Michael gathered up what wood he could find and added it to the campfire.

"Gonna fry us up some prairie chicken for supper," Quirk said.

"Check the beans," Quirk said. "Chicken is done."

Michael stirred the beans in the pot with a wood spoon. The stirring didn't slow the boiling, the sign Quirk said that they were cooked. "I think they're ready."

"Grab a plate. Let's eat."

After eating canned fruit and beef jerky for days the fried chicken and beans tasted wonderful, and Michael and Michele quickly ate their fill.

Quirk drank coffee with his food.

The twins drank condensed milk with water to thin it out. The mixture was sweeter than regular milk and delicious.

"Sir . . . Mr. Quirk, may I ask what you plan to do with us?" Michele said.

"I've been thinking on that," Quirk said. "There isn't a proper town I can take you to between here an' Omaha without my losing the entire herd. And seeing as how I can't exactly leave you here to the wolves or for Miller and his bunch to find there is only one thing to do that would be right."

"What is that, Mr. Quirk?" Michael said.

"Take you with me to Omaha."

"Omaha?" Michele said. "How long will that take?"

"With no more setbacks three weeks or so," Quirk said. "Maybe a bit less if one of you can learn to drive a wagon."

"Three weeks?" Michele said. "Our aunt . . ."

"It's the best offer I can give you," Quirk said. "Aunt or no aunt. She ain't here and I am, so we're stuck with each other until we get to Omaha."

Michael and Michele exchanged glances.

"Yes, sir. I mean Mr. Quirk," Michael said.

"Three weeks is a long time," Michele said.

"Not so long when you're your age," Quirk said. "When we reach Omaha, I'll wire your aunt and see what she wants to do with you. More than likely she'll want me to put you on a train to Chicago."

"What's in Omaha, Mr. Quirk?" Michele said.

"Stockyards, same as in Chicago," Quirk said. "Only my beef is for the army. Same for the horses. It's also a lot closer to Chicago than you are now. If your aunt wants you back in

Chicago, there's a train directly there I can put you on that will take no more than a few days. In the meantime you get three squares a day and you'll stay dry until we reach Omaha. And as I see it, a little hard work won't hurt you two educated pipsqueaks none."

Quirk stuffed his pipe with tobacco and lit it with a stick he set in the fire. He puffed and drank his coffee.

"Mr. Quirk?" Michele said. "What did you mean by hard work?"

"Well, I been losing time, seeing as how my cook died," Quirk said. "Got nobody to drive the wagon. I figure you can do that. Your brother can help me ramrod the herd. We all work and we all eat, and you get to go to Omaha and then home or to San Francisco."

"I don't know how to drive a wagon," Michele said. "We always had a taxi driver take us places."

"A taxi?" Quirk said.

"That's a man who drives a carriage to take you places," Michele said. "He usually charges a dollar, and then you give him an extra dime as a tip."

"What's 'ramrod,' Mr. Quirk?" Michael asked.

Quirk looked at Michael. "I suppose you never rode a horse before?"

"I've petted them, usually when the taxi picks us up," Michael said. "I gave one a carrot once."

"You gave one a carrot once?" Quirk said.

"He ate the greens and all."

Quirk sighed. "Well, tomorrow you two go to my school," he said. "All right, grab some blankets and make a bedroll by the fire. We'll be up by dawn with a full day of learning ahead of us."

While the twins made bedrolls of green wool blankets, Quirk added wood to the fire so that it would burn most of the night.

"Goodnight, you two," Quirk said as he settled into his bedroll.

"Goodnight, Mr. Quirk," Michael said.

"Thank you for taking care of me when I had the fever," Michele said.

"You're welcome," Quirk said. "Now you best get some sleep. Tomorrow is going to be a long day. For all of us."

# THIRTEEN

Seated on the buckboard, Quirk passed the reins to Michele.

"Give the reins a gently flick of the wrist to start the horses moving," Quirk said. "A tug to the left to make them turn left and the same to go right. Pull back to make them stop. That long stick by your side is the brake to lock the wagon in place. A horse is a herd animal. Once I get the herd moving, they'll just pull the wagon so as not to get left behind. Your main job is to make sure they don't step in no chuckholes and break a leg."

"This wagon is awful heavy Mr. Quirk," Michele said. "The horses . . ."

"Those are quarter horses," Quirk said. "They can pull three times their own weight. Together, this wagon is like hauling a dollhouse to them. So let's get this wagon rolling."

Holding the reins, Michele looked down at the two massive horses hitched to the chuck wagon.

Watching beside the wagon, Michael said, "Come on, Mikey, you can do it."

"You be quiet, Mickey," Michele said.

"Yeah, be quiet, Mickey," Quirk said. "Now come on, girl, we ain't got all day to do this."

" 'Ain't' is an improper word, Mr. Quirk," Michele said. "The proper words to use are 'don't' or 'do not' and the word 'start' instead of the word 'get' to make this wagon begin moving. My English teacher told us never to use the word 'ain't.' It speaks poorly of a person's education."

"You don't say," Quirk said. "Well, if your English teacher was here, I'd make her drive the wagon, but seeing as how she ain't . . . isn't, I guess you'll just have to do. Now quit your stalling and move out the wagon."

Michele took a deep breath and then flicked her wrist. It was amazing how easily the horses moved the wagon forward.

"Good, good," Quirk said. "Go about twenty feet and turn them to the left and then stop."

Michele pulled the reins gently to the left, and the horses turned in that direction. She let them go about twenty feet, then she pulled gently on the reins, and the horses stopped dead in their tracks.

"See? Nothing to it," Quirk said. "Now let's practice going a bit faster. The herd moves slow, but not that slow, and you have to keep up."

"Okay," Michele said.

After a bit more practice, Michele was able to control the horses at a moderate pace, and Quirk was satisfied she would be able to keep up somewhat with the herd. If he lost sight of her, he could always ride back until she caught up.

"Now you, boy," Quirk said as he stepped down from the buckboard.

"Now me what, Mr. Quirk?" Michael asked.

"This here horse belonged to my cook," Quirk said as he patted the small mare. "She's small and not too young, perfect for a boy of your size and lack of experience."

Michael looked at the horse. She towered over him and must have weighed a thousand pounds or more.

"Small, Mr. Quirk?" he said.

"My cook, Mr. O'Brien, was a rather small man, and he always rode a small horse," Quirk said. "He used a Mexican saddle as they tend to run smaller than American. Mexicans like to add silver to their saddles, and this one has silver buttons sewn onto it. You hold the reins and rub her neck while I get the saddle from the wagon."

Quirk walked to the chuck wagon and climbed aboard next to Michele.

"Is Mickey going to ride that horse, Mr. Quirk?" Michele said.

"Let's hope so, little miss," Quirk said. " 'Cause it ain't gonna ride him."

Quirk entered the wagon, removed O'Brien's saddle and horse blanket from under a wool blanket, and carried them out the rear of the wagon.

"First thing is to put the blanket on her back so the leather doesn't rub against her skin and irritate her," Quirk said.

Quirk placed the blanket over the horse's back.

"Now the saddle," he said, and draped the saddle over the blanket. "You reach under her belly and buckle the belts together so they fit snug, but not so tight she can't breathe. She'll need to breathe to run. She'll let you know right off if you made them too tight."

Quirk showed Michael how to loop and buckle the saddle belts so the saddle fit snugly and wouldn't slip while he rode her.

"Okay, rub her neck a bit like you were petting a dog or cat," Quirk said.

Quirk walked to his horse and removed his rope from the clip on the saddle. He made a loop on one end and gently placed it around O'Brien's horse's neck.

"Now put your foot in the stirrup there, grab the horn, and pull yourself onto the saddle," Quirk told Michael.

Michael placed his left foot in the stirrup and tried to reach the saddle horn, but he just wasn't tall enough. After several attempts, he slipped and fell on his rear.

"Come on, Mickey, you can do it," Michele said.

"You shut up, Mikey," Michael said.

"What's the problem, boy?" Quirk said.

Michael stood up. "The problem is that I'm short, Mr. Quirk, and I don't expect to grow any taller by the time we reach Omaha."

"I'll give you a boost," Quirk said.

With Quirk's assistance, Michael was able to grab the saddle horn and lift himself over and onto the saddle.

The horse immediately responded by nervously bucking a bit.

"Hey . . . hey . . . stop that," Michael said.

Holding the rope around the horse's neck, Quirk said, "Lean forward a bit and rub her neck to show her you mean no harm, and she'll calm down."

Michael leaned forward and rubbed the horse's neck.

"She's well trained and knows what to do," Quirk said. "She just has to learn she has a new boss on her back, is all."

After a few moments of being rubbed, the horse settled down.

"Now take the reins and gentle-like, give her a giddy-up," Quirk said.

Michael took the reins, gave them a gentle flick, and the horse moved forward. Quirk gave the rope some slack, and the horse walked in a slow circle around him.

"Give her a tug to the left," Quirk said.

Michael did, and the horse changed direction around Quirk.

"She'll do the work," Quirk said. "You just tell her what to do and where to go."

"How can I tell her what to do when I don't know what to do?" Michael asked.

"Good question," Quirk said. "So let's start learning."

★ ★ ★ ★ ★

For half the morning Quirk rode side-by-side with Michael and showed him how to turn, accelerate, stop on a dime, and herd the other horses and cattle into a tight-knit group and move them forward.

"Horses and cattle are herding animals," Quirk said. "They will always follow the leader. One of their own or us. In this case the leader is us. Once they start to follow, they won't stop until we do. Once they've stopped, they won't start again until we do, unless something or someone rattles them."

Once he was satisfied the boy was a quick learner, Quirk put Michael through the paces of riding ramrod over the herd. Michael took to the saddle and relaxed, and his horse soon knew exactly what to do when he wanted her to do it. After a while riding actually became fun, and Michael found the experience very enjoyable.

Until Quirk called a break for lunch.

And Michael dismounted.

And his back hurt.

And his neck ached.

And his legs felt like the rubber he used in school to correct mistakes.

"What's the matter, boy?" Quirk asked when he noticed Michael limping.

"My legs feel kind of weak," Michael said.

"You'll get used to it," Quirk said. "Build us a nice fire. Girl, get down off that wagon. We're going to go get us some eggs."

"Eggs?" Michele said. "From where?"

Quirk looked at the open prairie. "From the general store."

Michele looked out at the vast open range and scratched her head.

★ ★ ★ ★ ★

Quirk led Michele onto the prairie where the cattle and horses grazed on tall sweet grass. A few of the cows watched them, but most of the herd paid them no mind.

"Chickens on a farm or chickens on the prairie is still just chickens," Quirk said. "They roost and make nests."

"*Are* still just chickens, Mr. Quirk," Michele said.

"That's what I said."

"No, you said 'is,' " Michele said. "The proper word to use when referring to more than one is the word 'are.' They *are* still just chickens."

"Well, are or is, they do the same thing on a farm that they do on the open range," Quirk said. "They lay eggs."

"Out here?" Michele said.

"They's chickens, ain't they."

"They are . . . never mind."

"See that thick brush about a hundred yards yonder?"

"Yes."

"What do you see?"

"I see thick brush like the kind I hid in the other night when I got sick."

"You see brush," Quirk said. "I see a general store."

Quirk and Michele walked to the heavy brush.

"Sun's hot. Chickens like shade to lay their eggs," Quirk said. "Go on and stick your nose inside."

"My nose?"

"You got one, ain't ya? Or don't they teach you how to smell in your fancy school?" Quirk said. "Poke it on in."

Michele got down on her hands and knees and, carefully avoiding the thorns, poked her head into the brush.

Immediately a dozen or more chickens rushed out of the brush on the opposite end, clucking and squawking.

Michele stood up and looked at the chickens as they ran away.

"Why don't they fly?" she said. "They have wings."

"Chickens is a stupid bird," Quirk said. "They forget they can fly. All right, crawl on in and fill my hat with eggs. Leave them some, so they don't feel like they been robbed when they return."

Quirk removed his hat and gave it to Michele.

Carefully, Michele crawled into the brush. There were at least twenty eggs, maybe more, and she counted twelve and placed them in Quirk's hat. Then she backed out and stood up with the full hat.

"I got them!" she said excitedly. "A dozen of them."

"Good. You can carry them back. Careful you don't jostle them. Just hold on a minute while I grab a few of these."

Quirk inspected the thorns in the brush and selected and removed a handful of the longest ones and stuck them into his shirt pocket.

"Okay, let's go," he said.

By the time Quirk and Michele returned to the chuck wagon Michael had a good campfire going.

"Hop in the wagon and find Mr. O'Brien's big fry pan, the mixing spoon, the lard, and his mixing bowl," Quirk told Michael. "There's some measuring cups there. Fill one of his buckets with three cups of flour and bring out a can of condensed milk and the can of maple syrup. We're going to make us some flapjacks."

"My belly is about to bust," Michael said.

"Mine, too," Michele added.

Quirk loaded his pipe with tobacco and used a wood match to ignite it. He puffed smoke and looked at the sun.

"Mr. Quirk, why did you pick those needles from the brush?"

Michele said.

"Glad you reminded me," Quirk said and removed the thorns from his pocket. "My other socks have a hole in the toe and these make fine sewing needles in the absence of a real one."

"You sew?" Michael said, somewhat amazed.

"Out here there ain't no one to take care of yourself but you," Quirk said. "You don't learn how and things get awful messy real quick."

"Can you show us how?" Michele said.

"Maybe tonight when I change socks. Right now we got a solid six hours of daylight ahead of us," Quirk said. "I think we can make six or seven miles before dark. Girl, make sure everything is packed away in the wagon. Don't try to stay pace with me. The middle to the rear of the herd is fine. If I can see you, I can reach you. Boy, make sure the fire is good and out. We don't want to set fire to good grasslands and ruin it for the next herd coming through."

The sun was low in the sky when Quirk decided to halt the drive for the day, and he and Michael steered the herd into a green pasture of tall grass.

"We come as far as we can go for one day," Quirk said.

"How far is that?" Michael said.

"I figure nine miles. Let's tend to the horses," Quirk said. "Girl, climb down from the wagon and stretch your back a bit. Boy, let's tend to our horses, and then we'll make a fire and fix us some supper. Remember, a man always tends to his horse before himself. Without your horse, you'll die."

Under a blanket of a million stars, Quirk smoked his pipe and drank a final cup of coffee.

"Come tomorrow, we push east for three days to where the stream turns to the north," Quirk said. "That morning on the third day, we fill our four water barrels on the wagon and cover them tight. Canteens, too. That's our only water for eighty miles."

"Eighty miles," Michele said.

"Don't fret," Quirk said. "Those four barrels could last us a month if they had to. Best get some sleep. Dawn comes early, and we can't afford to dawdle in the sack like we was a bunch of eastern bankers."

"Mr. Quirk?" Michele said.

"What is it?"

"We have nine eggs left in the wagon."

"Then we'll have us some scrambled eggs and bacon in the morning," Quirk said. "Do you know how to make biscuits?"

"No, I don't," Michele said.

"Do you know how to eat them?"

"I do," Michael said.

"Good," Quirk said. "Then you can learn how to cook them."

★ ★ ★ ★ ★

# The Drive East

★ ★ ★ ★ ★

# Fourteen

On the first full day in the saddle, Michael thought his back would break wide open, it hurt so bad. He tried to keep up with Quirk. He knew Quirk was taking it easy because of him, so he tried not to show how badly his back ached as he sat tall in the saddle. He suspected Quirk knew anyway.

Michele's back hurt as well from sitting so long on the buckboard, but not nearly as badly as her hands hurt from holding and tugging on the reins for ten hours or so. What made the pain worse was the constant jarring of the wagon as it traveled over uneven ground. It seemed with each bump, her back would simply just fall apart. She would hold and pull the reins tighter, and the leather would dig into her soft hands, causing her much pain.

"Let's round them into a tight-knit circle in the tall grass so they'll stay put for the night," Quirk told Michael. "Girl, bring the wagon over to that little clearing by the creek. We'll camp there tonight," he told Michele.

While Michele drove the wagon to the designated spot beside the stream, Quirk and Michael guided the herd into the tall grass by riding around the cattle in a circle, drawing the circle tighter and tighter, until the cattle and horses were in one large grouping.

"A good day's work, son," Quirk said. "Let's tend to our horses. Always remember what I told you, you tend to your horse before you tend to yourself."

Quirk and Michael dismounted and walked their horses to the wagon.

"Remove the saddle and blanket and give her a good brushing," Quirk said.

Quirk showed Michael how to use the heavy horse brush to wipe the sweat and salt off his horse and remove tangles from her mane.

"You got to let a horse cool off slowly so they don't get sick," Quirk said. "As big a beast as they are, they're as delicate as people when it comes to sickness."

"Mr. Quirk?" Michael said as he brushed his horse.

"What is it, boy?" Quirk said.

"Does your back ever hurt?" Michael said. "From riding all day, I mean."

"When I was a boy first learning to drive a herd, my back hurt day and night. My neck, too," Quirk said. "I wasn't much older than you are now. Maybe fourteen or so. Thing is, after a while you get hard and then it don't hurt so much anymore. Either that or you just learn to ignore the hurt and get on with things."

"I think I'll just ignore it," Michael said.

"Wise decision. Check her hooves for breaks and splits in her shoes," Quirk said. "There's extra shoes in the wagon if one is broken or she loses one on the trail."

Michael looked at Quirk.

"Do like I do," Quirk said.

Quirk took his horse's right front leg, bent it backward, and held the hoof between his legs.

"Does that hurt him?"

"A horse's legs and knees bend backwards like so," Quirk said. "Just like us. And it doesn't hurt them any more than it would you."

Michael lifted his horse's right front leg and placed it between his knees.

"See any cracks in the shoe or pebbles stuck in there?" Quirk said.

"No."

"Then leave it be and check the others," Quirk said.

"Mr. Quirk?" Michele said.

"What is it, girl?"

"My hands are bleeding."

Quirk released the horse's leg and turned to Michele.

"Let me see."

Michele held her palms up for Quirk to inspect.

"Grab a bar of soap and wash them good at the creek," Quirk said. "I'll rub salve on them, and tomorrow you wear gloves."

Michele found soap in the wagon and a clean towel and went to the stream to wash her hands and face.

While she was gone, Quirk and Michael made a campfire. Dinner was beans, bacon, biscuits left over from breakfast, jerked beef, coffee, and condensed milk with water.

"Mr. Quirk, do you ever get sick of beans all the time?" Michael said.

"Nothing would please me more than to cut into a thick juicy steak right about now," Quirk said. "But a trail drive ain't for luxury, and that's for sure."

"How long have you been a cowboy?" Michele said.

Well, let's see now," Quirk said. "I started wrangling when I was fourteen or so, around 'fifty-five. After the war, I went to work for a ranch in Nebraska and drifted west. I started my own place in 'seventy-one outside of Casper. So, you might say it's been a while since I been anything else."

"You were in the war?" Michael said.

"Joined up with the First Infantry. They sent me to train in New York City in 'sixty-three," Quirk said. "A noisy, dirty place that New York. Too many people living in too small a place, if you ask me."

"And what did you do?" Michael said.

"This and that until early in 'sixty-four, when they formed what they call a sniper squad," Quirk said. "I was promoted to second lieutenant on what they call a field commission, and took a squad of sixteen men on special assignments all over the south."

"What's a sniper?" Michele said.

"Someone who is a crack shot with a long rifle."

"Was it exciting?" Michael said.

Holding his tin plate, Quirk looked at Michael. "No," he said. "Nothing is exciting about war. And there ain't no glory in it, neither. A lot of young men die and a lot of fat old men sit around and watch and grow rich."

"Mr. Quirk, do you have a family?" Michele asked.

Quirk looked at Michele. "No," he said softly. "And that's enough questions for one night. Get them dishes and pans down to the creek and wash them off while I gather up enough wood to last the night. I feel a chill in the air coming on."

Watching the stars overhead, Michele and Michael fixed their bedrolls close to the campfire, as it was, as Quirk said, a chilly night.

Quirk rested against his saddle and smoked his pipe.

"Mr. Quirk," Michele said. "Our Aunt Angela will be very worried about us by now. Is there any way to get word to her by telegraph?"

"Ain't a telegraph for a hundred miles," Quirk said. "Summerville ain't on the lines and probably won't be for years."

"They have the telephone in public places like the police and fire stations in Chicago," Michele said. "They say in five years people will have them in their houses. I know my aunt will."

"I read about the telephone a while back in the *Denver Star,*" Quirk said. "I can't say people will have much use for it except maybe for the gossipers."

"Our teachers at school say that by 1900, phones and electric light bulbs will be normal in almost every home," Michele said.

"What's an electric light bulb?" Quirk asked.

"Thomas Edison invented a glass bulb that gives off light by electricity and doesn't cause heat," Michele said. "He's a genius, our teacher said."

"Let me see Thomas Edison feed you out here in the wilderness," Quirk said. "Or your teacher, for that matter."

"I think Thomas Edison lives in New Jersey, Mr. Quirk," Michael said.

"Our teacher is in Chicago," Michele added.

"Enough talk about light bulbs and telephones," Quirk said. "Best get some sleep. We got a twenty-mile or more to drive tomorrow, and Thomas Edison and your teacher ain't here to help us."

Hours later Quirk opened his eyes and looked up at a billion stars and a bright moon. He didn't move a muscle as he listened.

To the crackle of the dying campfire as the last of the wood burned.

To the soft breeze as it blew overhead.

To the sounds of the night.

And the nervous whinnies and snorts coming from the cattle and horses.

And the low growls of a hungry wolf pack as it selected a kill.

Quirk sat up, grabbed his Winchester rifle, which was never more than an arm's length away, and stood up.

Slowly Quirk walked to the edge of the open range where the herd was on high alert. He scanned the darkness for shadows of the pack cast by the bright moon.

Michele woke first and saw Quirk walking to the herd. She nudged Michael.

"Mickey, wake up."

Michael opened his eyes. "What is it?"

"Look."

In the moonlight, Quirk spotted a pack of six or seven wolves as they moved in on a small cow. They sensed its smallness and weakness.

The alpha male led the chase to the cow. The pack followed and circled. They knew what to do.

Quirk took aim, fired a shot at the alpha male's legs, and the wolf jumped backward. Quirk then fired six more shots at the wolf pack, and they scattered into the darkness of the prairie.

Quirk stood very still for a moment, watching and listening. Then he removed bullets from his holster and reloaded the Winchester.

The night was silent.

The herd was not. They mooed and snorted nervously in the dark.

Quirk waited.

Minutes passed.

"Come on if you're coming," Quirk whispered.

And they came.

An all-out assault charge, led by the alpha male.

Quirk aimed carefully, waited for the alpha male to enter the moonlight, and then fired one shot. The wolf fell dead from a direct hit to the head. Sensing their leader was down, the rest of the pack turned and scattered.

For good measure, Quirk fired several more shots at the ground directly behind the pack, and they split up and disappeared into the night.

Quirk waited for the herd to fall silent and slowly walked back to camp.

Michael and Michele were standing with open mouths beside the fire.

Quirk saw the look of fear in their eyes and on their faces.

"It's nothing," Quirk said. "Just some wolves looking for an easy meal."

"Did you . . . kill it?" Michael asked.

"Just the boss. Had to. I can't afford to lose one more cow," Quirk said. "Back to bed. We won't see any more wolves tonight. Without their boss to tell them what to do, they'll retreat and regroup to elect a new boss."

Quirk showed Michele how to mix flour, water, and yeast to form dough. He showed her how to separate the dough into small balls and, after lining the large fry pan with a coating of lard, she set the balls into the pan, covered it, and set it into the campfire.

"Boy, you watch them biscuits," Quirk said. "Every few minutes lift the cover and check them to make sure they rise and brown good on both sides. Careful to use a towel to lift the lid or you'll burn your hands. Me and your sister are going to get some eggs."

Michael did as instructed. In fifteen minutes or so, the biscuits were fully cooked and he removed the pan from the fire.

While Michael watched the biscuits, Quirk and Michele walked out to the prairie and he let her select a bush to find eggs. On the third bush she tried, she found dozens of chickens and eggs.

A few minutes later Michele and Quirk returned with his hat full of chicken eggs.

They feasted on scrambled eggs, bacon and biscuits, condensed milk with water, and coffee for Quirk.

As they broke camp, Quirk looked at the horizon as if studying from a book. He knew the signs. He knew how much time before a storm hit and the destruction it would bring when it did.

"This time of year we can expect one major storm a week," Quirk said. "I see one now getting ready to brew sometime tomorrow."

"How can you tell?" Michael said.

"By the color of the sky and the way the clouds are forming," Quirk said. "Get mounted. We got twenty miles to make today. We'll be lucky to make any tomorrow."

"Mr. Quirk, somebody is coming!" Michael said.

Noon camp was to give the horses a chance to rest a bit and eat grain. Quirk rested against his saddle with a cup of coffee and peered at the approaching riders in the distance.

"I see them," Quirk said. "They've been dogging us since this morning."

"Is it Mr. Miller and his men?" Michele said.

"No."

"How can you tell from so far away without binoculars?" Michael said.

"By the way a man sits on his saddle," Quirk said. "I saw Miller sit atop his, and he ain't with this bunch."

Quirk estimated the riders were thirty minutes from reaching camp. He could move the herd and try to keep ahead of them, but they would only catch up. If their intentions were bad, he had the twins to think about.

"I need you two to do exactly as I say and ask no questions," Quirk said.

"Is something wrong?" Michele asked.

"That's a question and the answer is I don't know, but I aim to find out right quick."

"What do you want us to do?" Michael said.

Quirk looked at the chuck wagon.

Quirk stood several feet in front of the rear opening of the chuck wagon and watched the four riders slowly approach camp. They had the look of hard men used to a dishonest way of life. When you've met enough of them, they were easy enough to spot by the way they carried themselves. Squinting eyes with a look of desperation on their faces.

Quirk had the Winchester resting against his left leg and held a coffee cup in his right hand. His unlit pipe dangled between his lips.

The four riders stopped ten or so feet short of the chuck wagon.

"Hope you don't mind us invading your camp like this," the lead rider said. "We saw you from back a ways. Thought maybe you could spare some supplies."

"I'm running low myself," Quirk said.

"Sorry to hear that," the lead rider said. "You had a couple of people with you a ways. I don't see them now."

"They left," Quirk said.

"Ya don't say?" the lead rider said.

"I do say," Quirk said.

The lead rider scanned the prairie. "Which direction?"

"What is it you want?" Quirk asked.

"I told you, supplies."

"And I told you I can't spare any," Quirk said.

"What if we just shoot you and take what we need?" the second rider said. "Could you spare any then?"

"Go ahead and twitch, and you'll be dead before you hit the ground," Quirk said.

Two Winchester rifles slowly emerged from the rear opening of the chuck wagon.

The first rider looked at the Winchesters.

"You said they left," he said.

"I didn't say they went far," Quirk said. "Now ride out of here and keep riding while you're still breathing. I'm not in the mood for grave digging."

"This ain't over," the first rider said.

"Isn't," Quirk said. "Isn't over. 'Ain't' is an improper word."

"What?"

"Get going," Quirk said.

The first rider slowly moved his horse past Quirk. The second rider turned and looked at Quirk.

"See you soon," the second rider said.

"You best hope not," Quirk said.

Only when all four riders were well out of sight did Quirk tap on the side of the chuck wagon.

"Come on out now," he said.

Slowly Michael and Michele poked their heads out of the wagon.

"Were those men criminals?" Michele said.

"Cattle rustlers," Quirk said. "They ride the open ranges until they find a small outfit they can handle and then rustle the cattle."

"They're gone?" Michele said.

"Yes. Now come on out of there and gather your wits."

"Maybe we should wait and see if they come back?" Michele said.

"I'll know if they come back. Let's move out," Quirk said. "We'll camp early tonight, but I'd like to make at least six miles."

"Mr. Quirk, are these rifles loaded?" Michele said.

"Course not," Quirk said. "I wouldn't give a squirt like you a loaded rifle. Now just leave them be in the wagon and let's get a move on."

"I wish mine was loaded," Michael said.

"Don't be in such a hurry to get yourself killed before you have the chance to grow up," Quirk said.

# Fifteen

Around four in the afternoon, Quirk called a halt to the day's drive and settled the herd into a nice spot not far from the creek. He selected the spot because opposite the creek were some nice hills and steep rocks.

As Quirk and Michael tended to their horses, Michael said, "Mr. Quirk, what would you have done if those men tried to shoot you as they said?"

"They were at a disadvantage," Quirk said.

"How so?"

"They were on horseback," Quirk said. "If they draw their guns, they aren't the only thing that moves. Their horses move along with them. That requires extra time to cock, aim, and fire with any degree of accuracy. By then I will have shot two of them and beaded in on the others. They knew that, and that's why they moved along so quickly."

"We helped too, didn't we?"

"Sure did. Now gather up as much wood as your arms can carry," Quirk said. "And don't dawdle doing it."

Quirk built a nice fire and kept adding more and more wood to it as dark settled in so that the blaze could be seen from a great distance. After a quick supper, Quirk pointed to the tallest rocks beyond camp.

"See them rocks over there?" he said.

Michael and Michele turned and looked at the rocks.

"Grab a canteen of water and some jerked beef and head up

there," Quirk said. "Find a good spot to hide, and don't come out for any reason except I say so. Now go on."

"But Mr. Quirk, we don't want to leave you," Michele said.

"I wasn't asking," Quirk said. "Now do as I say right now. And make sure you stay hidden, and whatever you do be quiet about it. Real quiet."

"Come on, Mikey," Michael said.

Quirk waited until the twins were safely out of sight in the rocks and then he made three bedrolls stuffed with extra blankets and set them in the shadows beside the campfire.

Then he added all the available wood he could gather into the fire and picked up the Winchester rifle. He took a box of ammunition from the wagon and climbed the hill opposite the rocks where the twins were hiding. He scanned the rocks and was satisfied the twins were well hidden in the dark crevices.

A good hour or so of silence passed before Quirk heard the first soft rustle of a man on foot.

"Mickey, do you see anything?" Michele whispered.

"No," Michael whispered. "Now be quiet so I can see."

"I think you mean be quiet so you can listen," Michele whispered.

"Would you shut up," Michael whispered.

Leaning over the edge of the high rocks, Michael and Michele peered down at the blazing campfire.

"Mickey, can I tell you something?" Michele whispered.

"What?"

"Mickey, I think I love Mr. Quirk," Michele whispered.

"I'm right fond of him, too," Michael whispered. "Now will you shut up."

"No. I think I want to marry him," Michele whispered.

"Mikey, we're only twelve," Michael said. "Mr. Quirk is old like Aunt Angela. You can't marry him. People will think he's your grandpa."

"I can in a few years," Michele said. "You heard him say that he wasn't married."

"I heard, now be quiet," Michael said.

"I can't help it," Michele whispered. "I get this funny feeling in my stomach when I'm around Mr. Quirk. If that isn't love, what is it?"

"That's not love, that's the beef jerky acting up. Some bicarb will fix that right up. Now be quiet so I can hear."

"No, it's different," Michele whispered. "Like butterflies in my stomach."

"I wish you were a butterfly right now so I could swat you."

"Michael, I heard something," Michele whispered.

"Me, too. Be quiet."

The twins went still and peered down over the rocks.

Quirk avoided looking at the campfire to keep his night vision intact. He'd learned that trick a long time ago when the army sent him to special school to learn how to be a sniper. At night, avoid looking at a campfire and allow your eyes time to adjust to the dark, and your vision becomes more acute.

The same is true of your hearing.

A shadow moving inside a shadow tells a story, and so does a rustle of leaves on a windless night, or the snap of a twig underfoot.

So Quirk heard the soft snap of a twig many seconds before he saw the shadow of a man against the tall rocks and readied his mind for what was to come next.

The Winchester rifle was already cocked, and he held it loosely in his arms as he watched the shadows of the four men as they walked softly into camp.

Quirk could see their cocked pistols in their hands.

The four men surrounded the three bedrolls beside the campfire.

They aimed their pistols and fired several shots each into the bedroll. When the last of the shots echoed and faded away, one man reached down and yanked a blanket off a bedroll.

"Ain't nobody here," he said. "It's just blankets."

From the rocks, Quirk stood up. "One twitch and you're four dead men," he said.

The four men spun and looked up at the rocks, but Quirk was an invisible shadow lost in the shadows of many. They fired their guns at the rocks and Quirk shot one man, cocked the lever, and shot another.

"That's two," Quirk said. "Do you want to join your friends?"

The remaining two men stared up at the rocks.

"Toss your guns, and I'll allow you to walk out the way you came in, alive," Quirk said. "Otherwise you'll join your two companions on the ground there."

The two men tossed their revolvers to the ground.

"Belts, too?" one of them said.

"Naw, keep 'em, unless you plan on throwing the bullets at me," Quirk said. "Now walk out of here and keep this in mind. If I see you again I'll kill you on the spot and leave your bodies for the buzzards to peck your eyes out."

Slowly the two men turned and walked into the night. Quirk sat back and waited.

After several long minutes Quirk heard the sound of horses riding away, and he climbed down from the rocks and stood over the two dead men.

Quirk covered the bodies with blankets and then scanned the rocks above him.

"You two up there, come down and be careful doing it,"

Quirk said. "I don't need you breaking an arm or leg on me now."

It was morning by the time Quirk had dug two graves and buried the men. He removed their gun belts and kept their pistols, went through their pockets, and found a few dollars in folding money and some silver coins. Neither man had identification, so Quirk left the graves unmarked. The horses belonging to the two dead men were left behind. After placing the saddles and gear into the wagon, he set them free on the range. Most likely they would just follow along on their own accord.

"We should say a prayer over them," Michele said.

"Pray for men who would shoot you in your sleep and rustle your cattle?" Quirk said. "I don't think prayer would help where these two souls are going. I've wasted enough time on them already. Let's move out. We'll make it a short day, camp early, and get some rest before sunset."

Quirk swung his horse in an arc to guide the herd to the good grazing land beside the creek. Michael kept pace with him. When Quirk was satisfied the herd was happy he and Michael dismounted and walked their horses to the chuck wagon.

"Girl, get down from there," Quirk told Michele. "We're camping here until tomorrow morning."

Quirk secured the four water barrels to the shelves on each side of the chuck wagon with heavy rope. The covers fit snugly so water wouldn't spill as the wagon jostled on the trail or evaporate in the hot sun.

"We need to fill each barrel and all our canteens, as the creek turns north at this point and we don't," Quirk said. "And eighty miles is a long way to go to the next water if you ain't got none."

Michele drove the wagon close to the creek and, using a bucket, they formed a train. Quirk got into the stream with a bucket, filled it, and passed it to Michael on shore. Then Michael passed it to Michele, who dumped the water into a barrel.

It took about two hours of nonstop work to fill the four barrels.

"I don't know about you youngsters, but I could use a bath to wash the stink of those rustlers off me," Quirk said. "Girl, grab a bar of soap and some towels from the wagon."

Michele went to the wagon and found a dry bar of soap and some towels and took them back to the creek.

Quirk and Michael were stripping off their clothes.

"The water won't be none too warm, but it might be your last bath until we reach Omaha," Quirk said.

Michele stood and watched Quirk and Michael.

"What are you waiting for?" Quirk said.

"Mr. Quirk, I'm a woman," Michele said.

"A woman?" Quirk said. "You ain't but eighty-five pounds soaking wet on a full stomach."

"I have breasts Mr. Quirk," Michele said.

"You have . . . you ain't but twelve years old," Quirk said.

"I'm budding," Michele pointed out.

"Flowers bud," Quirk said. "You're just a squirt."

"I'll wait my turn, thank you," Michele said.

"Suit yourself," Michael said as he stripped off his pants.

"Michael, don't you dare get naked in front of me," Michele said.

"Then go wait in the wagon," Michael said.

"I will."

Michele turned and stormed toward the chuck wagon, climbed in the rear, and pulled the flap shut.

Michael picked up the bar of soap. "Women," he said.

Quirk sighed. "Come on boy, let's get clean."

Stripped of their clothes, Quirk and Michael dove into the creek headfirst.

"Damn, that's cold," Quirk said when he came up at the midpoint. "You got the soap?"

Michael held the bar of soap above the water.

"Scrub up and pass it along. Don't forget to wash your hair."

Michael scrubbed his body and then used the soap to wash his hair.

Quirk took the soap and did the same.

"Mr. Quirk, how did you know those men would come back last night?" Michael asked.

Washing his hair, Quirk paused. "Rustlers see an easy opportunity to steal a herd, they don't give up on it so quick," he said. "They murder and steal to get what they want. I've run across their kind many times before. A fox can't help being a fox and neither can rustlers."

Quirk dove into the water to rinse off and Michael did the same.

"Well, let's give your budding sister a chance," Quirk said as they climbed onto the embankment.

Rubbing a towel through his hair, Michael said, "Mr. Quirk, my sister is a little funny in the head."

"What do you mean?"

"Last night when we were hiding in the rocks she said she wanted to marry you," Michael said.

"She said what?"

"I told her she couldn't marry you because you're old, like our Aunt Angela."

Quirk looked at the chuck wagon. "Well that explains that," he said.

"What?"

"Nothing. Get dressed, and we'll fix us some lunch while

your sister takes a bath."

While Michele took a bath in the creek, Quirk and Michael hunted two prairie chickens for lunch.

Quirk showed Michael how to pluck the feathers without damaging the birds and then built a spit made of sticks. The chickens were roasting by the time Michele returned from the creek.

Quirk smoked his pipe and drank coffee while the chickens roasted.

"Son, turn those birds so they cook even. Careful you don't burn yourself," Quirk said.

Michael carefully rotated the chickens and then sat beside Michele.

"Twelve, maybe fourteen more days to Omaha, and then I'll wire your aunt and put you on a train to Chicago," Quirk said.

"And what happens to you?" Michele asked.

"Nothing happens to me," Quirk said. "I go home and start over for the next year's drive."

"All alone?" Michele said.

"I'll hire on a new cook."

"I mean, you live all alone?"

"Well, I wasn't always all alone," Quirk said. "Back in 'sixty-two before I joined the army, I had a nice little spread of eighty acres in Indiana," Quirk said. "I wasn't more than twenty-two years old back then and had me a pretty wife and a baby girl."

"You were married with a family?" Michele said, shocked to hear such news.

"Surprised?" Quirk said. "I wasn't always an old coot of a cowboy, you know."

"So what happened?" Michael asked.

"They had a one-room schoolhouse and I went to the eighth grade," Quirk said. "This girl in class named Allison Jane was a year younger than me, and the prettiest thing you ever saw. In that last year of school she came up to me one day and said 'Matthew Quirk, you will be my husband one day,' and two years later we were married."

"And what happened?" Michael said.

Quirk puffed on his pipe before he said, "We never thought the war would touch us in Indiana, but we were wrong. The Rebs came up from the south, the Yanks moved west, and fighting was all around us. That's when I joined up. I never thought they would take the war out on civilians. I couldn't have been more wrong on that account and many others."

"Who are they?" Michele asked.

"When I returned in 'sixty-six, Allison and the baby were buried in a field under a giant oak tree," Quirk said. "The house had been burned to the ground with them still in it. They told me Allison died protecting our baby from smoke."

"Who did it?" Michael said.

"I never found out if the Rebs or the Yanks were responsible," Quirk said. "No one knew. After that, I sold the land and moved west and maybe I have been alone all this time, but only in body. My wife and baby are always with me in spirit, you see. So I ain't truly alone so long as I carry their memory inside with me."

Michele turned her head so Quirk wouldn't see the tears running down her cheeks.

"But that was a long time ago," Michael said. "Why can't you find a new wife? You're not that old, and you're not ugly or anything."

"I don't expect you to understand this at your age, but I can't marry a second wife when I haven't forgotten the first one yet," Quirk said. "Maybe some day that feeling will change and I'll change along with it, but in the meantime I'm still married to Allison Jane in my heart."

Michele stood up and walked behind the chuck wagon so she could cry without being heard by Quirk.

Quirk puffed on his pipe and looked at Michael. "Flip them birds again so they don't burn," he said.

Michael rotated the chickens again and said, "I think they're done."

"Go fetch your sister and let's eat," Quirk said. "Then I'm going to do something no self-respecting cowboy would do in the afternoon."

"What's that?" Michael said.

"Take a nap."

Michael nodded. "I could nap," he said.

# SIXTEEN

Michele waited until she was sure Mr. Quirk and Michael were asleep before she got up from her blanket and wandered over to the field where the cows and horses were grazing on tall grass.

She was so distraught over the story of Mr. Quirk's family that she felt as if she would never sleep again. Never eat again. Never be happy again. There was a big, dark empty feeling in her stomach, and she tried her best to understand why it was there.

She sat in the shade of a tall tree.

What he said about carrying the memory of his wife and baby inside was exactly how she felt about her parents. Sometimes their memory was so alive, she felt as if she could see them, talk to them. Then the realization that they were gone would surface, the memory faded, and the pain in her heart returned.

All around her, cows and horses munched on the grass and wandered around, but then a fat cow standing alone suddenly collapsed to the ground as if she were hurt or sick.

Michele stood up and walked across the field to the fallen cow. She was bleeding, and heavily.

Michele ran all the way back to the camp.

"Mr. Quirk, Mr. Quirk, wake up!" Michele shouted.

Quirk and Michael opened their eyes.

"Mikey, what are you . . . ?" Michael said.

"One of the cows is sick," Michele said. "She fell down and she's bleeding."

Quirk stood over the fallen cow and stroked the stubble on his chin. "Well, she's looking to drop, but she ain't gonna do that on her back," he said.

"Drop what?" Michael asked.

"A calf, from the look of things," Quirk said.

"Do you mean she's going to have a baby cow?" Michele asked. "Right now?"

"That's precisely what I mean," Quirk said.

"She doesn't look too well," Michael said. "She looks sick."

"That's because she's having a problem," Quirk said. "She wants the baby out, but for some reason it wants to stay right where it is."

"We have to help her," Michele said.

"And I just had me a bath." Quirk sighed.

"Is she going to die?" Michael said.

"Not if I can help it," Quirk said. "The both of you strip down to your underwear, and I don't want to hear no nonsense about budding women."

Michael, Michele, and Quirk stripped down to their underwear.

"All right, girl, you get down beside her and rub her neck gentle-like," Quirk said. "Talk soft to her like you was telling a baby a story. Let her know we're here to help. Boy, get across her body and do your best to keep her from moving around too much."

Quirk knelt before the cow's rear and looked at the heavy bleeding.

Slowly, Quirk inserted his right hand into the cow and felt around. The cow mooed and struggled at his touch.

"Press on her, boy," Quirk said.

Michael pressed down on the cow to hold her steady.

Quirk removed his arm. It was covered in blood and dark slime.

"What is it?" Michele asked as she stroked the cow's neck.

"Cord is tangled around the baby's neck," Quirk said. "She wants to come out, but it's choking her."

"Can you help her?" Michele asked.

"I'm gonna try," Quirk said. "Keep doing what you're doing, the both of you. This may take a while before we're through."

Slowly Quirk inserted one arm and then the other. He felt around for the cord wrapped tightly around the calf's neck. It was choking the calf's airway and preventing it from moving forward.

Gently, Quirk started to unravel the cord from around the calf's neck. It was delicate work and slow going. A good hour passed before he felt the last of the cord come loose, and then he removed his arms.

"Come on now, do what nature intended," Quirk said.

A few minutes passed and Quirk said, "I can see her nose. Come have a look."

Michael and Michele sat beside Quirk and watched.

"I see it, her nose," Michael said.

"Why is it taking so long?" Michele said.

"You think this is long?" Quirk said. "Wait until you have one of your own. Time moves like molasses in wintertime when a woman is waiting to drop."

"Her head is coming out," Michael said. "Just like the time Aunt Angela's cat had kittens in the basement."

It took about fifteen minutes for the head to fully emerge. The eyes were closed, and it was covered in blood and slime, but breathing.

"Should we give her some help?" Quirk asked.

"Yes," Michele said.

"What do we do?" Michael said.

"Grab hold of her and pull," Quirk said. "But not too hard."

Michael and Michele took hold of the head and gently tugged. Slowly the shoulders appeared, then the front legs and stomach, and, with one mighty push by the mother, the entire newborn calf was in their lap.

Covered in blood and black slime, Michael and Michele didn't seem to mind a bit as they held the newborn in their arms.

"Congratulations," Quirk said. "You're aunt and uncle to a baby girl."

Suddenly, the calf stood up on wobbly legs.

"She's looking for her mama," Quirk said. "We best get her on her feet. You two stand back now and hold that calf still so she don't get hurt."

Quirk got down and took hold of the cow around the neck. He started to gently rock back and forth and the cow began to rock with him. After a dozen or so rocks the cow suddenly sprang up and looked around nervously for her calf.

"Let the baby go now, and nature will do the rest," Quirk said.

Michael and Michele released the calf, and the mother cow started to lick her baby clean.

Quirk sighed. "By God, I need another bath."

Quirk and Michael walked into camp where Michele sat, wrapped in a blanket and warming herself by the campfire.

"Two baths in one week," Quirk said. "Pretty soon I'll be wearing dude clothes and taking tea and cookies in the parlor with the spinsters."

"Mr. Quirk?" Michele said. "Can I ask you a question?"

Quirk sat and reached for his pipe.

"Go ahead," he said as he stuffed the bowl with tobacco.

"What happens to the cows when we reach Omaha?"

Quirk fished a match out of his shirt pocket, struck it against a stone, and then lit his pipe. "What do mean, what happens to them?" he said. "I sell them to the army."

"What does the army do with them?"

"Why, they use them to feed soldiers," Quirk said. "What did you think?"

"Even newborn babies?"

"I expect they'll wait a while on that," Quirk said. "What's troubling you, girl?"

"Somehow it doesn't seem right to have the army kill a mother and her baby after we . . . helped deliver it," Michele said.

Quirk looked at Michael. "You feel the same way, boy?"

Michael nodded.

"If this don't beat all," Quirk said.

Michele grinned at Michael.

"What should we have for supper?" Michael said.

"I know it ain't going to be beef," Quirk said.

Michele gently shook Michael until he rolled over and opened his eyes.

"Michael, I want to talk to you," Michele whispered.

"It's the middle of the night," Michael whispered.

"It will only take a minute."

"Well, what is it then?"

"Not here. I don't want to wake Mr. Quirk. Come behind the wagon."

Michael got out of his blanket and followed Michele behind the chuck wagon.

"What?" Michael said.

"Keep your voice down."

"All right, now what is it?"

"When we reach Omaha and take the train to Chicago, we should ask Mr. Quirk to go with us," Michele said.

"He has to go home," Michael said. "You heard him say that."

"I know. Just listen to me. If we tell him we're afraid to travel alone, he'll want to go with us to protect us," Michele said.

"But we're not . . ."

"To meet Aunt Angela."

"What for?"

"Think about it," Michele said. "She's alone. Mr. Quirk is alone. They're both old. They could get married. Then we wouldn't have to leave Chicago."

"I thought you wanted to marry him."

"That was before he told us about his family," Michele said. "How he never forgot his wife and baby."

"What makes you think he'll forget them in Chicago?"

"Mr. Quirk and Aunt Angela are both around the same age," Michele said. "She has to be lonely all the time just like Mr. Quirk. She's pretty, and if he shaves and gets a haircut and some new clothes, she might think he's handsome. Maybe together they'll think it's time to stop being alone?"

"Maybe you could be right," Michael said.

"Don't say anything until we reach Omaha."

"I won't."

"Promise."

"All right," Michael said. "Can I go back to sleep now?"

Michele spat on her hand and waited. Michael spat on his hand and they shook.

"Now you can go back to sleep," Michele said.

"I'll wash my hand first," Michael said.

# SEVENTEEN

Quirk pulled out the baking shelf on the chuck wagon and spread out his maps. He drank coffee while he studied them.

While Quirk studied the maps, Michael and Michele packed away their blankets and then put out the campfire by tossing dirt on it.

"Mr. Quirk, is everything all right?" Michele asked as she approached the chuck wagon.

"Just seeing where we are," Quirk said. "We crossed Nebraska yesterday, and I didn't even realize it. Are you two ready to go?"

Michele nodded. "About the cow and her calf?"

"Don't worry your pretty little head about it," Quirk said.

The cow and her calf tried to keep up with the herd for the first hundred yards, but the calf still had weak legs and, as the herd left them behind, they finally gave up and stayed put.

Quirk turned in the saddle and pointed to the mother and calf.

"They've given up," he said. "They'll stay behind and she'll raise her calf on the prairie. Both will wind up fat and happy and maybe find a stray bull or two."

Michael turned his horse and looked back.

"Mikey, look!" Michael yelled to Michele.

Michele stopped the wagon long enough to look back and then she smiled at Quirk. "Will they be all right?' she said.

"They're doing what God intended them to do," Quirk said.

The terrain changed a bit as they rode east through Nebraska. The land grew more flat and wide open and seemed to stretch out as far as the eye could see in every direction.

"They call this country the Great Plains," Quirk said. "On account of it being so flat and open."

Riding beside Quirk, Michael said, "We read about it in school."

"Reading about it in a classroom and crossing hundreds of miles of it on a horse are two different things," Quirk said. "Personally, I think riding through it beats reading about it any day."

Looking around at the vast, flat plains, Michael nodded. "It sure does," he agreed.

Shortly before noon, Michael spotted the band of followers on his right.

"Mr. Quirk, look," he said.

"I spotted them a few miles back," Quirk said. "Those are Arapaho dog soldiers."

"Indians?"

"They live mostly on the reservations in Wyoming and Colorado now, but there was a time when they roamed free all across the west," Quirk said.

"What do they want?" Michael said.

"Same as us," Quirk said. "Ride over to the wagon and tell your sister to stop where I do. We'll make camp and wait."

"Wait for what?" Michael said.

"Our friends to join us," Quirk said.

Quirk, Michael, and Michele sat in a circle around the campfire and looked at the thirty or so dog soldiers facing them on horseback a hundred yards or so away.

Quirk smoked his pipe and drank coffee as he studied them.

"What are they doing?" Michael asked.

"Waiting," Quirk said.

"Why?" Michele asked. "What are they waiting for?"

"See that big fellow in front there? The one with the chest plate and feathers?" Quirk said.

"I see him," Michele said.

"Who is he?" Michael said.

"His name is Red Scar, and he's the leader of that bunch. There was a time when you didn't want to tussle with the likes of him, but nowadays he's content to patrol the plains here and in Wyoming and relive the glory of the past."

"I don't understand," Michele said.

"I expect you don't," Quirk said.

"I think they're coming," Michele said.

"They are, and you two don't move or say a word unless I tell you to move or speak. Understand?"

Quirk continued to smoke his pipe as Red Scar led his men toward Quirk's camp. They stopped and formed a circle, and Red Scar dismounted. He made the sign for greeting by touching his chest with his right hand and then moving it in an arc from left to right.

Quirk stood and made the same gesture.

Red Scar spoke in his native language of Algonquian.

"What's the matter, cat got your tongue, you old buzzard?" Quirk said.

Red Scar stared at Quirk.

Michael and Michael exchanged glances and then looked at Quirk.

"He speaks English better than me, and French and some Dutch, to boot," Quirk said. "He's just speaking Algonquian to aggravate me, is all."

Red Scar slowly smiled at Quirk.

"Do you have smoking tobacco?" he said.

Hearing his deep, booming voice, Michael and Michele went wide-eyed.

"Course I do," Quirk said. "What do you think is in my pipe, old newspapers? Sit down. Have a pipe and some coffee."

"Do you have sugar?"

"You know damn well I do."

Red Scar walked to the fire and sat cross-legged in front of Michael and Michele. From under his vest he pulled out a well-worn corncob pipe.

"Who are these children?" Red Scar asked.

"I picked them up on the trail," Quirk said. "I'm taking them to Omaha with me and putting them on a train to Chicago."

Red Scar nodded. "I've been to Chicago. I didn't like it much. Too many people. Too many tall buildings. The streets smell of horse dung. No place to ride a horse or hunt."

Quirk passed his tobacco pouch to Red Scar.

"Nice pouch," Red Scar said.

"Keep it, you bandit," Quirk said. "I have another."

Red Scar filled his pipe and tucked the pouch under his vest.

"The old days are gone, Quirk," Red Scar said. "In the old days I would have killed you and taken these children as my slaves."

"In the old days I would have shot you at a thousand yards and been done with your worthless carcass," Quirk said.

Red Scar grinned.

Quirk grinned.

The twins swallowed hard.

"Thank God the old days are gone, huh, Quirk?" Red Scar said.

"That is for sure," Quirk said. "So, how much do you need this time?"

"Four cattle and six horses."

Quirk nodded. "Will you ride with us a while?"

Red Scar nodded. "Until night. I enjoy frightening children in the night," he said and looked at the twins.

"Stop your nonsense and have your men go pick out the cattle and horses," Quirk said. "Then we need to talk private. You two kids go with them and make sure they don't cheat us."

"Us?" Michele said.

"With them?" Michael said.

"Go on, they won't bite you if you behave yourselves."

Red Scar spoke to his soldiers in Algonquian.

Michael and Michele stood up and looked at the dog soldiers. Two of the dog soldiers held out their hands. Michael and Michele reached up, and the dog soldiers lifted them onto the backs of their horses.

Quirk and Red Scar walked a bit past the chuck wagon, each puffing on their pipes.

"I picked those kids up last week on the prairie where they was running away from a nasty bunch who kidnapped them off a train," Quirk said. "They were going to sell the kids back to their family for money. They call that ransom. I met up with that bunch before I knew who they were. The leader calls himself Miller. He's riding with four or five others. Have you seen them in your recent travels?"

Red Scar removed the pipe from his mouth and looked at Quirk.

"No," Red Scar said. "Stealing the children of your enemy to keep as your own is one thing, but what those men did is something they should be put to death for. If we run across them, we will kill them for you."

"Appreciate that," Quirk said. "Want that cup of coffee?"

"That milk in a can, do you have that?"

"That I do."

"In that case, I will have some."

Quirk and Red Scar walked to the chuck wagon where Michele sat at the ready.

"This noble savage is going to ride with us a ways," Quirk said. "He wants to ride in the wagon with you."

"With me?" Michele said.

"He likes to drive wagons," Quirk said. "Personally, I think he's a nothing but a big kid at heart."

Red Scar climbed aboard and sat next to Michele. Without looking at Red Scar, she passed him the reins.

"Best hold onto your hair," Quirk said with a grin. "Red Scar is also fond of little girl's hair. Especially golden hair. He likes to decorate his vest with it."

Quirk turned and walked toward his horse.

Red Scar smiled at Michele.

"Hey, wait!" Michele yelped after Quirk.

Quirk and Red Scar stood side-by-side and looked at the horizon as the sun started to slowly set.

Each man had a cup of coffee and a pipe in hand.

"Where you headed from here?" Quirk said.

"North and then to the west," Red Scar said.

"I'll see you on the next drive," Quirk said.

Red Scar nodded. "Maybe I'll come see you on your ranch in the fall. I'll bring you some Nebraska corn."

"Come ahead," Quirk said. "It's about time you learned what it feels like to sleep in a bed."

"I have slept in a bed in a fine hotel in Washington," Red Scar said. "I didn't care for it much."

Quirk nodded. "What's troubling you, my friend?"

"Reservation life, no matter how big the reservation may be, is not what the Arapaho People were meant for," Red Scar said.

"You were meant for war, I know that," Quirk said. "But there ain't no wars left to fight, and there ain't nothing left to win even if there was one worth fighting."

"Sad," Red Scar said. "These times."

"I agree, but it would make me happy to one day be a nice old man and have you visit me on the ranch," Quirk said. "We'll sip whiskey, smoke our pipes, and eat Nebraska corn."

"See you in the fall," Red Scar said and extended his right hand to Quirk.

Quirk, Michele, and Michael stood and watched as Red Scar led his dog soldiers into the plains, where he disappeared into the setting sun.

"He's a fine old warrior," Quirk said.

"How did you become friends?" Michele asked.

"Back in 'seventy-three, or was it 'seventy-four? Anyways, old Red Scar and his soldiers tried their best to kill me on the plains, and I did my best to kill him," Quirk said. "After a while we got sick of shooting at each other for no good reason and decided it was easier on both of us to just be friends. Twice a year on the drive, I let him have some beef and horses, and he takes care of any potential Indian raiding parties that might be off the reservation for me."

"You mean he acts like a guardian angel?" Michele asked.

"That's one way to put it," Quirk said.

"What's the other way?" Michael said.

"It gives him something to do besides sit on the reservation, get fat, and wait to die," Quirk said. "If you two ain't got any more questions, I'd like to eat and get some sleep."

# EIGHTEEN

Michele felt the wagon suddenly wobble. A few moments later, the rear left wheel broke and the chuck wagon crashed, lopsided. Michele nearly fell off the buckboard.

"Mr. Quirk!" she yelled.

Forty yards or so ahead of the wagon, Quirk and Michael turned their horses around and spotted the busted wheel. They rode back to the wagon.

"Something's happened," Michele said.

"That something is a busted wheel," Quirk said. "Come on and get down. It's going to take a while to fix it."

"This is going to get messy," Quirk said. "Best strip down to your undershirts again."

Michael and Michele removed their shirts. Each wore a long-sleeved undershirt underneath.

Mounted under the wagon on a heavy lug nut was a spare wagon wheel, a pot of grease, and a support jack. From inside the wagon, Quirk removed a wood case full of tools. Then he got under the wagon to free the wheel and support jack.

Lifting and supporting, removing the broken wheel, replacing it with the new one, and greasing it down took the better part of two hours. Quirk and the twins were covered in grease by the time the wagon was ready to travel again.

"Mr. Quirk, all this grease," Michele said.

"I know it," Quirk said. "Only thing to do is boil a pot of

water and wash it off as best you can with soap."

Quirk filled a bean pot with water and made a fire to boil it. He filled a second pan with cold water. When the water in the bean pot boiled, he dipped in a small towel, lathered up a bar of soap, and washed his hands and arms and then his face.

Michael and Michele did the same and, while they weren't exactly squeaky clean, they were able to put their shirts on and handle things with a firm grip.

"We best not break another wheel," Quirk said. "We have two hundred-plus miles left to Omaha, and no spare."

Quirk spread his maps out by the campfire and ran a finger along a route marked in heavy dark pencil.

"Two days' ride to the next water," he said and showed the twins where they were and where they were going. "Then about two hundred miles into Omaha, and we're home free. We can make camp at the river for a day and give the herd a rest and us, too."

Michele traced a line from Omaha to Chicago. "How long does it take to go from Omaha to Chicago on the train?"

"I'm not sure," Quirk said. "Appears to be three days at least. We should have you home in two weeks."

"Do you think our aunt knows we're missing by now?" Michele said.

"I'm sure she does," Quirk said. "She's probably gone to the US Marshal for help by now. She'll be that much more relieved when you two turn up safe and in one piece."

"What about Mr. Miller?" Michael said.

"Omaha has a federal marshal," Quirk said. "We can tell him your story, and I'm sure he'll act upon it."

Michael traced his finger along the route to Omaha. "Next stop is home," he said.

"Next stop is going to bed," Quirk said.

Quirk kept a close eye on the darkening sky on the horizon. He'd seen that kind of sky before. It was ugly and brought out the worst in nature. He feared the worst was on its way, and they would be in the middle of it when it struck.

He called an early noon. By the time he had a campfire going, the dark sky in the distance started to show lightning.

"I don't like what I'm seeing in those storm clouds," Quirk said.

Michael and Michele looked at the horizon.

"A thunderstorm?" Michael said.

"I ain't sure just yet," Quirk said.

The horses and cattle, sensing the pending storm, started to form tight-knit groups.

Quirk watched lightning bolts strike the earth about a mile or so away.

"Put that fire out right now," Quirk said and walked to the wagon.

"Is something wrong?" Michele said.

"I think we're in for it," Quirk said and unhitched the team from the wagon.

The dark clouds grew darker and traveled across the sky quickly in swirling, ominous patterns.

The horses and cattle started to move about on the range.

"You two come here right now," Quirk said.

Quirk's horse started to pace nervously, and Quirk grabbed the reins to hold him steady.

Michele and Michael stood beside Quirk. They watched the sky as lightning flashed inside the clouds and a few bolts struck the ground a half mile away.

"Mr. Quirk?" Michele said.

"Quiet, hon," Quirk said.

A few drops of rain fell.

Quirk looked straight up at the sky as it broke open.

The rain fell harder, and suddenly the raindrops became balls of hail.

Quirk scooped Michele up and put her on the saddle of his horse.

"Hold on tight to the horn," Quirk said as he mounted the saddle. Then he reached down and grabbed Michael and lifted him onto the saddle behind him. "Hold onto my stomach and don't let go for no reason whatsoever."

Quirk looked at the sky as the tornado funnel touched down a few hundred yards down range.

The wind blew furiously in a spiral motion.

The cattle and horses scattered in every direction.

"All right," Quirk said and thumped his horse with the stirrups. "Show me something."

Quirk's horse took off and Quirk raced him several hundred yards down range. Then he stopped and turned around.

The tornado blew across the range with furious anger, destroying everything in its path.

"Headed our way," Quirk said.

"What is it?" Michael said.

"A twister, son. A tornado. And we don't want to get in her way, or she'll suck us into her funnel."

Quirk turned his horse and raced it several hundred more yards down range.

"She's turning direction," Quirk said.

They watched as the powerful tornado spread across the range. It seemed to grow stronger and angrier with each passing second, chewing up and destroying everything in its path. Then it weakened and broke apart and finally disappeared, and the ground went still.

Immediately things went calm.

"Stay put," Quirk said and dismounted.

Quirk held the reins and slowly walked his horse a few yards. Holding the reins, Quirk knelt down and inspected the clearing sky.

"I believe she blew herself out," he said.

Holding the reins of his horse, Quirk walked into camp with the twins beside him.

The wagon was on its side, although it appeared undamaged. The herd was scattered in every direction for up to a mile.

"It could have been a lot worse," Quirk said. "Let's get that wagon upright."

Quirk tied a rope around his horse and knotted the opposite end to a metal rib in the chuck wagon. Michele held the reins while Quirk and Michael stood to the side of the fallen wagon.

"When I say go, you walk my horse forward," Quirk said.

Quirk and Michael took hold of the wagon and Quirk said, "Go on now, and walk him forward."

Michele held the reins and walked the horse while Quirk and Michael lifted. Slowly the chuck wagon rose off the ground and rolled back onto four wheels.

"Well, there's nothing more we can do today except check our supplies and make camp," Quirk said. "Tomorrow we'll gather up the herd again."

Seated in front of the campfire, Michele said, "Mr. Quirk, how did you know a tornado was coming?"

Eating beans and bacon from a plate, Quirk paused and sipped some coffee. "Nebraska is flatlands of open range for the most part. I've seen many a twister this time of year on a drive. After a while you get to know the signs of one coming. Mostly the air goes still and the sky looks a certain way, like trouble is brewing."

"We don't have tornados in Chicago," Michael said. "We have a lot of wind and snow, but no tornados."

Quirk nodded. "Sometimes it's best to be grateful for what you don't have," he said.

By midmorning Quirk and Michael had rounded up most of the herd into one tight group. Once the herd was settled and grazing, they rode off to search for stragglers.

Michael spotted the downed horse first and pointed.

"Mr. Quirk, look!" Michael said.

They rode to the horse and dismounted. The horse was alive and suffering.

"What is it, Mr. Quirk?" Michael said.

"Running from the storm she broke her front leg," Quirk said.

"Can we help her?"

"Afraid not," Quirk said. "All we can do is ease her pain."

"How?"

Quirk drew his Colt Peacemaker and cocked it.

"Best look away now, son," Quirk said. "Some things ain't worth remembering."

"You're going to shoot her?" Michael said. "Can't you save her or at least . . ."

"Afraid not, son."

"But she's alive."

"I know it's a hard thing to think about, but to leave her suffering here on the plains is a worse thing," Quirk said. "Wolves and coyotes will eat her while she's still breathing. Now look away."

Michael turned around and Quirk fired his gun twice.

A moment later Quirk wrapped his arm around Michael's shoulder.

"Come on, we got a herd to drive back to your sister," Quirk said.

"It's a fine morning for driving a herd," Quirk said. "Are you two ready?"

On the buckboard, Michele said, "I'm ready, Mr. Quirk."

Mounted beside Quirk, Michael said, "Me, too."

"Then let's go to Omaha," Quirk said.

★ ★ ★ ★ ★

# The Abduction

★ ★ ★ ★ ★

# Nineteen

Frank Miller and Frog sat at a corner table in the Lucky Dollar Saloon in the town of Summerville and drank beer that came from the tap.

"We covered sixty square miles without a trace of those brats," Miller said. "I just don't understand it. I just don't. They're just kids, for God's sake."

"Maybe they got picked up or something?" Frog said. "Or fell to a wolf pack?"

"Maybe."

"But you don't think so?"

"I don't know what to think," Miller said.

"You going to send another wire to the aunt?" Frog said.

"I'm going to have to," Miller said. "We can't keep looking forever. She's just going to have to understand the brats brought this on themselves and we did our best to find them."

"I don't think she's the forgiving type," Frog said.

"I don't pay you to think," Miller said. "And forgiveness has nothing to do with this. They took it upon themselves to hop the train in the middle of the night. If she squawks, I'll tell her it was her fault for sending them away in the first place. They were brokenhearted at being sent away and decided to run off. What can the rich spinster do if the blame is on her?"

Frog sipped his beer.

"When will the boys get here?" Miller said.

"Tomorrow sometime."

Miller sighed. "All this trouble over a pair of brats."

"I thought it was over the money," Frog said.

Two dusty cowboys entered the saloon and walked to the bar. They ordered beers.

Miller looked at the pair. They were like most every other trail-worn cowpuncher he'd come across: lean, hungry-looking, and wearing trail dust for clothing.

Except these two were different.

They sipped their beers and stared at nothing, making no conversation.

And then Miller realized what was different about these two. They wore empty holsters.

Both of them.

Then they spoke loudly, and Miller couldn't help but overhear one say to the other, "If I ever run across that old cowboy again, I'll punch his ticket for him but good."

"Frog, see those two cowpunchers at the bar, the pair that just came in?" Miller said.

"I see them," Frog said. "What about them?"

"Something strike you as wrong about them?" Miller asked.

"Wrong? What do you mean wrong?"

"Take a good look."

Frog stared at the two men for a while and then he said, "Empty holsters, right?"

"Right," Miller said. "Go to the bar and tell them I'd like to buy them a drink at our table. Whatever they want."

"What for?"

"Just do as I ask."

Frog went to the bar and stood beside the two cowboys.

"Excuse me, gentlemen, but my friend and I would like to buy you a drink at our table," Frog said.

The two cowboys looked at Frog.

"You would, huh? Why?" one of them said.

"Ask my friend. It's his idea," Frog said.

The two cowboys looked at Miller, and Miller raised his beer glass to them.

"Okay," the cowboy said. "I could use a free beer."

Frog and the two men walked to Miller.

Frog took a chair.

"My name is Frank Miller. Why don't you men take a seat and order whatever you'd like on me," Miller said.

"First I'd like to know why you want to buy us a drink," one of the cowboys said.

"I think you might have an interesting story to tell me about why your holsters are empty," Miller said. "What are your names?"

"Kruk."

"Douglas."

"Sit. Order whatever you'd like and tell me what happened to your sidearms," Miller said.

Sipping the most expensive rye whiskey in the saloon, Kruk said, "This no-good bushwhacker of a cowboy drew down on us from the rocks when we came riding into his camp. Shot our two friends and accused us of trying to steal his herd. We didn't even get to keep their horses, and we could have sold them in town for traveling money and new sidearms."

"You surrendered your guns?" Miller said.

"Three Winchesters drawing down on you from the high ground, what would you do?" Douglas asked.

"Why do you care, anyway?" Kruk said. "Do you always take such an interest in the business of others?"

"I'll tell you my reasons in a moment," Miller said. "First tell me what this cowboy looks like."

"Tall fellow, rugged-looking, kind of sandy hair," Kruk said. "Had no trouble pulling the trigger, I'll tell you that."

"How big was his herd, would you say?" Miller said.

"Small," Douglas said. "Couldn't a been more than a few hundred head and a hundred or so horses at best."

"And he had two companions with him?" Miller said.

"Unless he had six pairs of hands," Kruk said.

"Did you see them?" Miller asked.

"No, but we sure saw them aim their Winchesters at us," Douglas said.

"Now tell us why you're so interested," Kruk said.

Miller reached for his wallet, flipped it open, and set it on the table.

Kruk and Douglas stared at the wallet.

"So what?" Douglas said.

"You can't read," Miller said.

"What of it?" Douglas said.

"It says that I am the owner and chief operating officer of the Illinois Detective Agency in Chicago," Miller said. "That cowboy you ran across is wanted for questioning by us for a possible crime."

"What's that got to do with us?" Kruk said.

"I want you to take me and my men to him, that's what it has to do with you."

"Say we do that, what's in it for us?" Douglas said.

"You mean like a reward?"

"That's exactly what we mean."

"We'll be arresting that cowboy and his associates," Miller said. "It would be a shame to see a good herd of cattle and horses go to waste out there on the prairie with no one to see to them. Maybe you two wouldn't mind taking care of that situation?"

Kruk and Douglas exchanged glances.

"Let me get this straight," Kruk said. "We take you to this cowboy, you arrest him, and we get to keep his herd, no questions asked?"

"Keep it, sell it, do whatever you want with it. He won't be needing it anymore," Miller said. "Just so long as you take me to him."

"All right Mr. Detective Agency, you got a deal," Kruk said.

"Good," Miller said. "We'll leave at first light. Have you a place to stay tonight?"

"We just rode into town," Douglas said.

"Have you money for the hotel?" Miller said.

"We were planning on sleeping at the livery for fifty cents," Kruk said.

"I'm going to give you some money for the hotel and for each of you to buy a new sidearm," Miller said. "I can't expect a man to lead us on a posse unarmed."

"Maybe you can throw in some eating money?" Kruk said. "We could use a good meal at that hotel."

"No heavy drinking," Miller said. "We start right after breakfast, and I want you fresh."

Miller and Frog had a nightcap of brandy in Miller's top-floor room at the hotel.

"I'm not getting this, Frank," Frog said. "We can find that cowboy on our own accord. What do we need those two cattle rustlers for?"

"We need them precisely because they are cattle rustlers," Miller said. "Think about it for a moment. If Quirk did come across the brats after we left him, he knows their story by now. He was going to Omaha. He'll put them on a train north to Chicago. That means when we intercept him, we'll have to dispose of Mr. Quirk because he's a witness to our business transaction. A witness who could do us a great deal of harm if he were left to talk."

"But what does that have to do with those two saddle bums?" Frog said.

"Everything," Miller said. "Even with Quirk out of the way, his herd will still be out there. Somebody will come across it. Somebody will trace his brand. Somebody will want to know what happened to Quirk. A federal marshal or the army out of Omaha, but somebody. Those two rustlers remove the herd and thereby the evidence that Quirk ever existed. And if something blows up and goes wrong down the road, it's on them as cattle rustlers."

Frog nodded his head and smiled.

"And once we have the brats, we'll take them to that ghost town. Then I'll wire Mrs. Dunn from Medicine Bow that we found them, but we need to pay the ransom," Miller said. "It's life or death, you see, so the ransom gets upped to one million per brat."

Frog grinned and held his brandy glass out to Miller. They clinked glasses and then downed their brandy.

"See you in the morning," Miller said.

"What about the rest of the boys?" Frog said.

"They'll be here or we leave without them," Miller said. "Either way, we go right after breakfast."

# Twenty

Miller reserved the largest table at the hotel for breakfast. Frog, Deeds, Pep, Houle, and Ferris joined Miller over breakfast. Miller carefully explained his new plan as they ate.

"Where are Kruk and Douglas?" Miller asked Frog.

"Over at the gunsmith picking out new sidearms," Frog said.

Miller nodded. "After breakfast, Frog, you and Pep hit the general store and load up on supplies. We'll move out as soon as everybody is packed and geared up."

"Here they come," Frog said.

Kruk and Douglas entered the dining room and walked to the table. Each man had a new Colt revolver in his holster.

"Gentlemen, these are our guides," Miller said. "Mr. Kruk and Mr. Douglas."

"Do we have time for breakfast?" Kruk said. "We had to wait for the gunsmith to open his shop."

"More than enough time," Miller said. "My men and I are finished here, but we have some last-minute details to cover. Have breakfast and meet us in front of the hotel in one hour. The bill for breakfast goes on my room, so order whatever it is you want."

"Listen up," Miller said an hour later when everybody met in front of the hotel. "We have a day's ride south and two days to the east before we catch up with Quirk. It shouldn't be too difficult to run down a slow-moving herd on the open range, but I expect every man to act professionally and follow my orders. Now Mr. Kruk and Mr. Douglas, mount up and lead the way."

By nightfall they'd traveled south far enough to intersect the path traveled by Quirk's chuck wagon.

Miller dismounted, knelt, and inspected the deep tracks in the grass made by the heavy wagon.

"It's them," Miller said. "Make camp. We'll pick up the trail in the morning."

From the better part of a mile away they could see the buzzards circling overhead.

"Think he lost some of his herd?" Frog said.

"Looks that way," Miller said.

They rode the mile and discovered a pack of coyotes feasting on a dead horse.

"Something happened here," Frog said.

Miller inspected the terrain from the saddle. "I'd say Quirk ran smack into a twister, by the looks of the flattened grass and debris," he said. "Can't be more than two days ahead of us at this point."

"Two sets of horse tracks with riders," Frog said. "One of them is probably driving the wagon."

"I told you he had two others holding Winchesters on us," Kruk said. "It has to be them."

"Mr. Kruk, I believe you," Miller said. "We won't catch them standing around here talking though. Let's ride."

"No water for another two days," Miller said as he inspected the wagon tracks. "They took on water, which weighed down the wagon some extra. That will slow them down even more. My guess is they'll camp a day to rest at the next watering place, and that is where we'll surprise Mr. Quirk and company.

Any questions?"

"We got two hours of daylight left, Frank," Frog said. "What do you want to do, ride on a bit or make camp?"

"Ride an hour and then make camp," Miller said.

About an hour later, Frog and Miller dismounted and studied the wagon tracks in the grass.

"Fresh," Frog said. "And the grass ain't been grazed on. The cowboy is pushing hard to the next water."

Miller and Frog stood up, and Miller studied the plains in front of him.

"Make camp and grab some sleep," Miller said. "We'll ride after dark. We'll find Mr. Quirk by moonlight."

"Mr. Quirk, look!" Michael shouted from atop his horse.

"That is what they call the Rainwater Basin," Quirk said. "Good water and plenty of it. We're just south of the Platte River. It's a good place to camp and rest the herd and us for the next day or so."

"Mr. Quirk, can I take a bath?" Michele said from the buckboard on the chuck wagon. "I smell like axle grease."

"I expect we all could use a bath," Quirk said. "Let's get the cattle in one place and make camp. I expect a day's rest will do everybody some good."

The eight-acre pond Michele waded in to was warm and not too deep. She scrubbed up with the bar of soap and washed her hair. By the time she had dried off, dressed, and returned to camp, Quirk and Michael were plucking the feathers off two wild chickens they had hunted on the plains.

A campfire roared, and a spit of sticks was over the flames ready for the birds.

"I figure we give the herd a rest for a day and us too," Quirk said.

The chickens were ready for roasting. Quirk slid sticks into them and set them over the campfire.

"How long to Omaha, Mr. Quirk?" Michele asked.

"No more than a week or eight days," Quirk said. "Come and watch these birds while we go wash up."

"Everybody dismount," Miller said.

The group dismounted and looked across the dark plains at the tiny red dot of a campfire about a mile away.

"From here we walk," Miller said. "We hobble the horses the last hundred yards and go in quiet. I don't want to take any chances of alerting this cowboy. And for God's sake, nobody hurt those kids. Anybody does, even by accident, and I'll shoot you where you stand."

Quirk opened his eyes when the barrel of a rifle pressed against his cheek. His first thought was of the safety of the twins.

"Twitch. Cough. Sneeze. Move a muscle, and you won't live to see a new day," the man holding the rifle said.

It was too dark to see the man's face, but Quirk recognized the voice.

Frank Miller.

"Get those kids out of their bedrolls," Miller said.

Frog and Deeds grabbed Michael and Michele from their bedrolls. They held the twins tightly around the neck and mouth so they couldn't move or shout.

"Now, cowboy, get up real slow and toss that Colt, and remember what I said about moving a muscle," Miller said. "And keep in mind if you try anything, the brats get it first and you get to watch."

Quirk slowly stood up with the rifle still pressed against his cheek. With his right hand he removed the Peacemaker from his holster and tossed it aside.

"Mr. Kruk, Mr. Douglas, do you have something you'd like to say to Mr. Quirk?" Miller said.

Kruk came up behind Quirk and grabbed his arms. Douglas stood in front of Quirk and punched Quirk in the stomach.

Michael and Michele tried to scream. Frog and Deeds smothered them to keep them quiet.

"Thought you'd seen the last of us," Douglas said and punched Quirk in the stomach again and again.

Quirk folded and lowered his head.

"He ain't so stout as I thought," Douglas said.

Quirk spit and said, "Why don't you try it alone with my hands free?"

"I don't think I'm inclined to do so. What do you think of that?"

Douglas was about to punch Quirk again when Quirk suddenly hit Douglas in the jaw with the top of his head, knocking Douglas backward to the ground and nearly into the fire.

As Douglas hit the ground, Quirk stood and flipped Kruk over his shoulder.

Douglas attempted to stand, but Quirk punched Douglas three times in the face, knocking him to the ground again.

On all fours like a dog, Kruk looked at Quirk just as Quirk kicked him in the face.

Miller stuck his long Colt pistol in Quirk's face.

"That's enough of that, cowpuncher," Miller said and cracked Quirk across the jaw with the heavy Colt.

When Quirk opened his eyes, the glaring sun was in his face. A gag made from his neckerchief was tied tightly around his mouth. His hands were tied behind his back with coarse rope. His legs were tied at the ankles.

A campfire was boiling coffee in his pot.

Miller and his men were drinking coffee from his cups.

On the opposite side of the campfire the twins were roped and gagged in fashion similar to Quirk.

"We can make Silver Springs in four days if we push it," Miller said. He looked at Kruk and Douglas. "Do you boys want the chuck wagon?"

"We'll take what supplies we need," Douglas said. "We don't want the wagon."

"We'll split the supplies and burn the wagon," Miller said. "Mr. Quirk won't be needing it anymore."

Kruk looked at Quirk. "What about him?"

"We'll take the brats," Miller said. "You do with him as you wish once we've gone, but wait for us to leave."

Douglas grinned at Quirk. "Hear that, cowboy? You're ours to do with as we wish, and I owe you for that butt to my jaw."

"Frog, you and Deeds go through the wagon and take what we need," Miller said. "We got a long ride ahead, and I don't fancy doing it on an empty stomach."

Bound and gagged, Michael and Michele were tied to Michael's horse.

"If you kids want to live to see the dawn, you behave yourselves and do exactly as I say," Miller said. "If you do that, you'll be back in Chicago and living the good life with your rich aunt. If you don't, well, just use your imagination."

"We're all set, Frank," Frog said. "Extra horse is loaded with supplies and water."

Miller looked at Quirk. "*Adios,* cowboy. Thanks for the grub and for taking such good care of the brats."

Kruk and Douglas waited for Miller and his bunch to vanish on the plains, then went through the wagon and removed all the supplies and water they could carry on horseback.

"Now look here, cowboy, at what I got," Kruk said. He held up the can of kerosene oil he found in the wagon.

Standing beside Quirk, Douglas laughed.

Kruk removed the plug from the can and splattered kerosene on the chuck wagon. He dug a wood match out of a pocket, struck it against the wood railing of the wagon, and tossed it onto the canvas top.

Immediately the wagon burst into flames.

"That takes care of your wagon," Douglas said to Quirk. "Now it's time to take care of you."

"Hold on a minute," Kruk said. "See what he has for identification. We go riding into Omaha saying we're working for him, we better be able to prove it to the army. I ain't riding all that way to leave empty-handed."

Douglas grabbed Quirk and yanked him to his feet. With his wrists and ankles tied, there was nothing Quirk could do to stop Douglas from emptying his pockets.

"Got a nice folding wallet," Douglas said as he riffled through the worn, leather billfold.

"Come on, hurry up," Kruk said. "We're wasting daylight."

Kruk removed the folding money from the wallet and shoved it into his shirt pocket. Then he removed a folded piece of paper, opened it up, looked at it, and turned to Kruk.

"You read better than me. What's this say?" Douglas said.

Kruk took the paper and stared at it for a moment, forming the words silently with his lips.

"Looks like a bill of sale for the army," Kruk said. "And that will do just fine.".

Douglas grinned at Quirk.

"Mister, it's time we had us a little ride," Douglas said.

Douglas went to his horse, removed the rope from the saddle, and took it to Quirk. He grabbed Quirk's bound wrists and tied one end of the rope around them and held the other end as he mounted his horse.

Quirk stared at Douglas as Douglas wrapped the other end of the rope around the saddle horn. Then, with a flick of the reins Douglas raced his horse forward, dragging Quirk along on the ground behind them.

Douglas ran his horse across the field, zigzagging back and forth, rolling Quirk over and over until he finally stopped at the edge of the pond where Quirk landed into the water facedown.

Douglas watched as Quirk didn't move in the water.

"Nobody tells me to drop my gun in the middle of the night," he said. "Nobody."

Douglas waited for thirty or so seconds, then satisfied Quirk wasn't getting up, he turned and ran his horse back to Kruk.

"He's done," Douglas said. "Drowned in the pond."

"You sure?" Kruk said.

"He ain't breathing, and I ain't wasting sweat burying him. Leave him for the coyotes and buzzards. Let's move," Douglas said.

# Twenty-One

Quirk waited for the sound of the herd moving out. Then he rolled over in the water and gasped loudly for air.

He was battered and bruised and maybe had a busted rib or two, but able to inch his way onto shore without causing himself too much pain.

Quirk sat and waited to catch his breath. Being dragged across the ground had loosened the knots in the rope around his wrists. Slowly, he was able to remove the bonds. Once his hands were free, he untied the rope around his ankles and stood up.

A knife-like pain shot through his left side, and he paused to breathe slowly and wait for it to subside.

Busted ribs for sure, or at least severely bruised from being dragged across the rough terrain.

Quirk looked at the still-burning remains of his chuck wagon and slowly limped to it, hoping to find something he could use in the ruins.

Most of what was left burned in the initial fire. As he rummaged through charred remains, Quirk found a large kitchen knife that he stuck in his empty holster, a full canteen, and several jerky sticks still intact.

There was a decision to make. Pursue the rustlers and try to get the herd back, or try to track down Miller and his bunch.

The rustlers went east to Omaha.

Miller went southwest to Silver Springs. The ghost town was

four or five days' ride and more like ten or more on foot.

If he had adequate food and water and didn't have bruised ribs, he might be able to make the walk. In his present condition, it was an impossible undertaking. Even if he did make it, Miller would have moved on by the time he arrived.

It seemed to Quirk that his only chance of catching Miller was to catch up to the rustlers and somehow get his horse and guns away from them. That also seemed like an impossible undertaking in his present condition.

However, those rustlers were stupid, lazy men to be sure. They would ride slow and camp early. He could overtake them in ten or twelve hours or so, if he walked at a steady pace.

Much easier said than done when just breathing hurt.

Quirk checked the direction the rustlers drove the herd and the placement of the sun, and, with one painful step, he started walking with one thought in mind.

Save those youngsters.

At any cost.

Even your own life.

"As soon as those brats are finished eating, tie them back up," Miller said. "I want to make another ten miles before dark."

Watching the twins, Frog nodded to Miller.

Drinking coffee, Miller returned to the campfire where the rest of his men were still eating noon chow.

Sitting on the ground next to Michael, Michele set her plate of beans down and leaned over to whisper in his ear.

"Hey, you two, quit the whispering," Frog said. "This ain't no church meeting."

"My sister is afraid," Michael said.

"Tell her to be afraid with her mouth shut," Frog said. "Or I'll put that gag back in and shut her up myself."

Michael looked at Michele, and she nodded.

Quirk estimated that he walked a mile or maybe a bit more. He had to stop and rest, as his ribs were on fire and the pain was causing shortness of breath and slight dizziness.

He sat in the soft grass, nibbled on a jerky stick, and washed it down with a few sips of water. Then he forced himself to stand and get moving again because he feared that if he stopped for a longer period of time, he would die alone on the vast plains and the worst would befall the twins.

Because if he died, he was almost certain the twins would die at the hands of Frank Miller.

That thought spurred him to get moving again and to keep moving.

Michael and Michele were allowed to ride Michael's horse with their hands free. A rope was slung around the horse's neck and tied off on Frog's saddle horn to keep them in close tow.

"Mr. Frog, wait! Please!" Michele suddenly cried.

Frog slowed and turned around.

"What is it?"

"My brother suffers from dizzy spells," Michele said. "We have to stop for a moment. Please."

Frog pulled up close to Michael's horse. The boy was slumped forward in the saddle with his eyes closed.

"What's the matter with him?" Frog said.

"I told you, he has dizzy spells," Michele said. "They come and go. It's been that way since we were little. We brought his medicine, but we left it on the train."

"Hey, Frank!" Frog yelled to Miller who was in the lead. "Problem."

Miller turned his horse around just in time to see Michael fall from the saddle to the ground.

The pain in his side was now so great that it didn't bother Quirk anymore. Like that toothache he once had that lasted for several months. By the time he saw a dentist in Casper, the ache was so familiar a thing it was as if it no longer was there. It was that way now with his ribs. Once Quirk got used to traveling with the pain, it no longer bothered or hindered him all that much.

He stopped for some jerky and water. He needed to keep his strength up if he was to keep moving most of the night. He checked the position of the sun in the sky, the tracks made by the herd, and then kept moving forward.

Michael was on the ground with Miller and his men standing around him.

"What is it, boy?" Miller said. "If you're faking this, I'll cut your tongue out and leave it for the buzzards."

Atop the horse, Michele said, "He isn't faking. He's had these spells since he was little. Look at him. You can see he isn't faking."

"Aw, hell," Miller said when he looked closer at the boy.

"We got just a half hour of daylight left, Frank," Frog said. "We might as well make camp and wait for the squirt to come around."

"All right, make camp," Miller said. He looked at Michael. "Remember what I said about your tongue."

The moon was up and cast just enough light for Quirk to follow the tracks of the herd left behind in the grass.

He kept walking, oblivious to the time, the distance, and the pain. After a while they all became the same thing.

Then he saw the red dot of a campfire, and he took a short rest and sat on the grass. He sipped cool water from the canteen, spat some on his hand, and dotted his face with it to remove sweat. He could ill afford to get sweat in his eyes when he needed clear vision.

He watched the red dot on the black horizon.

Maybe a mile to the rustlers, maybe a bit more.

Quirk stood up and started walking toward the red dot and watched it get closer with each passing step.

Miller pulled Frog aside from the campfire and the other men so they wouldn't hear him.

"Is the kid faking it?" Miller asked.

"Hard to tell with squirts like him, Frank. It could be true he has these spells. After all, he is a city kid. They tend to be soft and sickly a lot."

"Watch him close tomorrow," Miller said. "I have the feeling they're up to something, those two, and I don't like it."

"I'll watch them, Frank," Frog said. "Don't worry."

"Good," Miller said. "When we reach Silver Springs, I'll send Deeds and Pep in to scout it out before we ride in. I want to make sure it's totally deserted before we walk into some crazy old-timer's shotgun who thinks we're trying to steal his silver mine."

"How long you figure we'll have to keep them kids?" Frog asked.

"I've been studying on that," Miller said. "After I wire the aunt in Chicago, it's going to take her a week to transfer money into cashable bonds and ship them to Medicine Bow by train. That's another three or so for the train to arrive, and five days or so for us to put them on the train. We'll have to make sure they never reach Chicago."

Frog stared at Miller.

"It's the only way," Miller said.

"I don't kill children, Frank."

"Would you do thirty years in Yuma for them?"

Frog sighed. "No, not for nobody."

"Pep and Deeds will escort them back to Chicago," Miller said. "We will tell the aunt the rest of us went to track down the kidnappers. You and I will be on the same train and, before it reaches Chicago, we will have to eliminate the four of them."

"Kill Pep and Deeds?" Frog said. "I can't do that, Frank. We worked together for years. I know them too well to kill them."

"Just think about thirty years of hard time in Yuma, or one million in your pocket if you sacrifice a few sheep to the wolves," Miller said.

"And Houle and Ferris?"

"We'll bury them in Silver Springs along with the other ghosts."

Frog stared at Miller.

"And me?" Frog asked. "Do I wind up as one of your sheep on a train or buried in a ghost town?"

"Only if you cross me," Miller said. "But you wouldn't cross me, would you, Frog?"

Quirk came upon the campsite on his hands and knees. The fire was nearly out, but bright enough for him to see Douglas and Kruk asleep inside their bedrolls about twenty feet in front of him.

Quirk slid the long kitchen knife out of the holster and placed it between his teeth.

Slowly he started to crawl the twenty feet to the sleeping rustlers. He hoped and prayed the Good Lord would forgive his act of cold-blooded murder, but it was the only way he saw possible to save the two youngsters. It seemed a fair exchange of souls to Quirk, and he hoped the man upstairs saw it the same way he did.

Kruk was closest. As Quirk crawled to the man, he removed the knife from between his teeth and held it in his right hand.

Kruk heard the whisper of Quirk's movements as Quirk held the knife high overhead. Just as Kruk reached for his gun, Quirk slammed the knife directly into the rustler's throat.

Douglas was instantly awake. As Quirk pulled the knife from Kruk's throat, Douglas fumbled inside his bedroll for his gun.

Quirk charged Douglas.

In the pale light of the dying fire, Douglas saw hate, anger, and revenge in Quirk's eyes.

Just before Quirk reached Douglas, Douglas freed his gun, cocked, and fired wildly. The bullet grazed Quirk's left side, and it was as if a million lit matches touched the injured ribs all at once.

Douglas tore out of the bedroll and cocked his piece again, but Quirk charged and grabbed Douglas's arms. The two men wrestled wildly. For a few seconds they were locked in a motionless dance of looming death, but even wounded, Quirk was a formidable foe and the far stronger man. After a few seconds of hard struggle, Quirk slowly bent Douglas's arm backward and the gun fell from his grasp.

Quirk used his reserve strength to bend Douglas over backward until Douglas almost touched the ground. Quirk shoved the long knife into his chest directly over the heart.

Quirk released Douglas and the man fell dead to the ground.

Exhausted, in unbelievable pain, Quirk fell onto his back, gasped for air, and waited for the fire in his ribs to go out.

There was nothing left to do now but wait for daylight to break.

If he lived through the night to see it.

# Twenty-Two

"Michael!" Michele shouted as he fell out of the saddle.

Frog turned his horse around. "Frank, it's the kid again."

Miller dismounted and furiously walked to Michael.

"Get up, you little snot." Miller seethed with rage. "Or I'll take a whip to your ass but good."

"I can't get up," Michael said. "I'm too dizzy."

"We'll see about that," Miller said.

Miller returned to his horse and dug a slice of rope out of a saddlebag and took it to Michael. None too gently, Miller grabbed Michael and shoved him back onto the horse. With the rope, Miller tied Michael's hands to the saddle horn.

Miller looked at Michele. "If he falls one more time, I'll make you walk tied behind this horse the rest of the way."

Quirk opened his eyes. He had fallen asleep between two dead men. He looked at the blue sky above and for a moment he wondered if he had died, because there wasn't any pain in his side or his head or anywhere else.

Then he took a deep breath and the pain in his ribs was like a hard kick from an angry mule.

Slowly Quirk sat up and, holding his injured ribs, he made it to his feet. First things first. He reached for a canteen of water and drank until his thirst was quenched. Then he went through the supplies, found some jerky, and ate that standing up.

Feeling slightly stronger, Quirk looked around at the herd.

The cattle were scattered here and there on the prairie. A hundred yards away he spotted his horse. The saddle was still on him.

Quirk gave a loud two-pause whistle. Recognizing the signal, his horse turned his head and trotted to him. His Winchester was still in the sleeve on the saddle. Quirk rubbed his neck and went through the saddlebags for some sugar cubes.

"Now you stay put a moment," Quirk said.

Moving slowly, favoring his left side, Quirk gathered up as many supplies as he could fit into the saddlebags. Then he riffled through the pockets of Kruk and Douglas and took back his folding money and army papers. In Kruk's bedroll he found his Peacemaker and holstered it.

"Hold still so I can get on," Quirk said to his horse.

Grabbing the saddle horn, Quirk placed his left foot in the stirrup, fought through the pain in his side, and mounted his horse.

"Okay, let's go," Quirk said. "And I would appreciate it if you didn't step into any prairie-dog holes along the way."

# TWENTY-THREE

Miller called for a brief stop around one in the afternoon to feed and rest the horses and fill the bellies of the men.

"Give the horses some grain and fix us up some hot grub," he told his men. "Frog, how are the brats?"

"Girl seems to be okay, but the boy doesn't look so good," Frog said. "I don't think he's faking it, Frank."

"Cut him loose and let him get some rest," Miller said. "I don't want him dying on us before we reach Silver Springs."

By early afternoon Quirk arrived at his burned-down chuck wagon. The fire had gone out last night, but the air was heavy with the stink of smoke and charred wood. He had smelled many such an aroma during the war when attached to Sherman. The general had burned everything in his path on his march through Georgia to the sea.

Quirk dismounted and removed the saddle from his horse.

"Take a breather, and I'll do the same," Quirk said.

Using the saddle as a backrest and pillow, Quirk looked up at the blue sky until his eyes grew heavy and he nodded off to sleep.

Quirk awoke with a stiff back and his ribs on fire. He went through the saddlebags, found the pint bottle of whiskey still intact, and took two stiff swallows. The whiskey burned his throat and started a bonfire in his belly, but after a few moments the pain in his ribs lessened to a manageable point.

He dug out a few pieces of jerky and ate them with a few more sips from the whiskey bottle.

"Okay," Quirk told his horse. "Let's burn some daylight."

The hot afternoon sun beat down on the back of Quirk's neck and as much as he wanted a sip of water, he knew drinking while sweating would only make him thirst even more.

"A couple more miles before dark," Quirk told his horse. "Then we both can rest and take a few sips."

And he rode on, exhausted, in pain, weak and thirsty.

And then a strange and wonderful thing happened. Nothing hurt anymore, and he was no longer hot or thirsty. Just the opposite. He felt fine. Even a bit cold. And no wonder. Soft snow was starting to fall in front of his eyes, all beautiful and white. He watched the flakes dance and flutter on the breeze, and he reached out to touch them.

"Look here, boy," Quirk said to his horse. "Snowing in the summertime."

The sky went dark, the moon and the stars came out, and the softly falling snow danced around them. Quirk felt himself float away on a soft white cloud.

And he looked up at the millions of stars and snowflakes gently falling, and he drifted off on a nice, warm blanket of soft air.

Miller drank coffee as he paced around camp.

"What's eating at you, Frank?" Frog asked.

"Time," Miller said. "We're not making good-enough time to suit me. Houle, Ferris, you boys go on ahead tomorrow and scout that ghost town. If there's a problem, ride back and catch us on the trail. I hate surprises, especially the kind that interferes with my plans."

"Sure, Frank," Houle said. "I'm sick of riding with these brats anyway."

Miller glanced at the twins. They were tied back-to-back near the campfire.

"Untie them and give them something to eat," he said. "We need them alive, if only for a little while longer."

Quirk opened his eyes when his horse nudged him with his nose.

It was dark. He'd been out for a few hours at least. He must have passed out, fallen to the ground, and dreamt of the snow and stars.

"You're absolutely right," Quirk said. "Enough of this lazing about like we was bankers on holiday."

Quirk tried to sit up, but the searing white hot pain in his ribs was just too much, and he fell onto his side.

The horse nudged Quirk again. He looked up at the reins dangling over his eyes and understood.

"Good idea," Quirk said.

He took hold of the reins and pulled on them. The horse took a few steps backward, and slowly Quirk rose to his feet.

He slumped against the saddle, gasping in pain and for air.

"Just let me catch my breath and I'll be right with you," Quirk said and stroked his horse along his neck.

He took hold of the saddle horn, placed his left foot in the stirrup, and tried to pull himself up and onto the saddle, but the pain in his ribs was just too great, and he fell to the ground on his back.

"Sorry, old boy, but I think I've reached the end of it," Quirk said. "I don't have the strength to remove the saddle, but maybe a passing stranger will see fit to take you in."

He looked up at the billions of stars overhead. This time they were real, and then he slowly closed his eyes for what he was sure was the last time. "I'm sorry, youngsters," he said and passed out cold.

"Ride hard and you could make the ghost town inside of two nights," Miller said. "We should be a day, maybe a day and a half behind you. If you don't ride back to meet us, I'll assume everything is okay and we'll ride in."

Houle and Ferris mounted their horses.

"See you in a few days, Frank," Houle said.

Miller and Frog watched them ride out of camp.

"Hey, Frank, come have a look at this kid," Deeds said.

Miller turned and walked to the twins. They were tied back-to-back once more, and Michael's head was slumped forward against his chest.

"I don't care if he's sick or not, put him on their horse and tie his hands good," Miller said. "We've wasted enough time on this nonsense as it is."

Quirk opened his eyes with a loud gasp and tried to sit up, but Red Scar placed his hands on Quirk's bare chest and gently pushed him back onto the blanket.

Quirk's chest was wrapped tightly in white linen.

"Scar?" Quirk said.

"I see you've had some trouble since we parted ways," Red Scar said.

"That's putting it mildly," Quirk said. "What happened?"

"My scouts told me they spotted a group of men riding south," Red Scar said. "I thought it might be the men you spoke about."

"They were. How long was I out?"

"By your time, about thirty-six hours since we found you."

"Thirty-six . . . I have to get going," Quirk said and tried to sit up.

"You're not strong enough yet," Red Scar said.

"They have them kids," Quirk said. "They'll kill them for sure."

"And if you kill yourself trying to save them?" Red Scar said. "Everybody dies."

Quirk sighed and wiggled into a seated position. "Who bandaged my ribs?"

"I did," Red Scar said. "Are you hungry?"

"As long as I been out, I ought to be."

Red Scar turned and looked at his dog soldiers gathered around a campfire. He spoke to them in Algonquian, and a soldier filled a bowl with stew from a large cauldron and took it to Quirk.

"Eat," Red Scar said.

The bowl had a hand-carved wood spoon in it and Quirk took a spoonful of stew.

"When you finish, we'll talk," Red Scar said.

Quirk and Red Scar walked along the plains smoking their pipes.

"I'm grateful to you, Scar," Quirk said. "For saving my life."

"I had to," Red Scar said. "I enjoy aggravating you too much to let you die. And besides, who else will give me free beef?"

"My herd is east of here," Quirk said. "Probably scattered to the winds by now."

"I will send ten soldiers to gather them up and hold them for you," Red Scar said.

"I appreciate that," Quirk said. "In the morning I'll be riding after them."

"We will go with you," Red Scar said.

"They will kill those kids for sure if they see a war party on their tail led by me and you," Quirk said.

"You'll ride up against six men alone?"

"It won't be the first time," Quirk said. "It's what the army trained me to do, and I did enough of it during the war. What they call guerrilla warfare, you see."

Red Scar stared at Quirk for a moment. "You are willing to take on six men alone to save two children that aren't your own. Why would you do that?"

Quirk puffed on his pipe and watched the smoke blow away on the breeze.

"When I returned from the war, my wife and baby girl were buried in the yard of what was left of our farm," Quirk said. "To this day, I don't know who killed them, and I guess it doesn't really matter much anymore who. What does matter is that I wasn't there to save them. It wasn't my fault they got caught up in the war, but I failed them nonetheless by not being there."

Quirk paused and looked at Red Scar.

"Those kids won't die because I'm not there to save them," Quirk said. "I won't fail them the way I failed my family. Not this time. Not those kids. Not as long as I draw breath, that won't happen."

Red Scar nodded at Quirk. "If you don't make it, if they harm those children, my soldiers and I will kill them all for you."

"That's a kind offer, Scar," Quirk said. "In return, if I don't make it, you can keep my entire herd and property. I'll put that in writing before I leave."

"I will keep the herd, but we have no use for your property," Red Scar said. "Your government wouldn't allow us to keep it anyway, even if we had."

"Probably true," Quirk said. "It looks like your soldiers rustled up some nice turkeys for supper. How about I make us a nice pot of coffee?"

"Do you have any sugar left?" Red Scar said.

"If I don't, I can sweeten the pot with some three-dollar-a-bottle sipping whiskey from my saddlebags," Quirk said.

"Both would be good," Red Scar said.

Miller removed the ropes from Michael and Michele's wrists so they could eat by the campfire.

"If you behave yourself tomorrow, I won't tie your hands," Miller said. "But if you try to run, I'll give you a whipping you soon won't forget."

Michael looked at Miller.

"Mr. Quirk will come for us," Michael said. "And when he catches up to us, you'll be sorry for this. All of this."

"Look, you little snot, Quirk is dead," Miller said. "Those two rustlers we left back there with him, why do you think I brought them along in the first place? Now shut up, eat your supper, and no more talk about that old dead cowboy."

"He's not so old, and he scares you, doesn't he?" Michael said.

"I told you to shut up," Miller snapped.

"I can see it in your eyes and hear it in your voice. You're afraid of him," Michael said. "And you should be."

"Michael, be quiet," Michele said.

"Listen to your sister, runt," Miller said.

"I may be a runt and a city kid like you said, but at least I'm not a coward like you," Michael said.

"You little snot," Miller said and grabbed Michael in his left hand and yanked him to his feet. "I'll teach you to sass me," he said and slapped Michael several times across the face.

"Stop it!" Michele shouted and jumped to her feet.

Miller tossed Michael at Michele, and they stumbled to the ground.

"You'll go to bed hungry," Miller said. "Frog, tie them up. Tight."

★ ★ ★ ★ ★

"My medicine man wants to check your bandage," Red Scar said.

Quirk was seated at the campfire, and he stood up. "Does he speak English?"

"Not so much," Red Scar said. "He's learned some good cuss words from the whites assigned to supply beef to the reservation if you'd care to hear them."

"Tell him for me his medicine is good, and I'm grateful," Quirk said.

Red Scar told the medicine man, who nodded and replied.

"He said to remove your shirt," Red Scar said.

Quirk nodded to the medicine man, unbuttoned his shirt, and removed it. Carefully the medicine man removed the wrap from around Quirk's chest.

The lower ribs on Quirk's left side were swollen and purple. Ever so gently, the medicine man touched them. Quirk winced in pain.

The medicine man spoke to Red Scar.

Red Scar nodded and said to Quirk, "He wants to put medicine on your ribs to ease the pain."

"What kind of medicine?" Quirk asked.

"Medicine man secret," Red Scar said. "He would never reveal it except to another medicine man."

Quirk looked at the medicine man. "Tell him okay."

Tied back-to-back, Michael and Michele sat in the shadow of the dying campfire. Miller and his men were in their bedrolls asleep.

"Michael," Michele whispered.

"What?"

"Are you okay?"

"I think so, yes."

"Michael, what if it's true what he said about Mr. Quirk?"

"Don't think that way."

"But what if it is?"

"I don't know."

"Do you know what I think, Michael?"

"What?"

"I think Mr. Miller has no intention of ever letting us go. I think when he gets his money, he'll kill us because we know all about what he did. He has to know we'll tell on him the first chance we get otherwise."

"Yeah, I think you're right."

"We have to try to escape."

"When?"

"The first chance we get," Michele whispered.

"Whatever he rubbed on me stinks to high heaven," Quirk said as he sat before the campfire and smoked his pipe.

"That's why my soldiers are all sleeping downwind," Red Scar said.

Quirk turned and looked past the fire. The dog soldiers were all far enough away from him that they couldn't smell the salve the medicine man rubbed on his ribs.

"It helps though, doesn't it?" Red Scar said.

"I have to admit it does, although now that I smell it, I don't think I want to know what's in it."

"Can you ride tomorrow?"

"I can and I will."

Smoking his own pipe, Red Scar nodded. "You are a foolish and stupid man, Quirk."

"If someone stole your herd, kidnapped two innocent children in your care, and left you for dead, what would you do?" Quirk said.

Red Scar looked at Quirk.

"I guess we are both foolish and stupid men," Quirk said.

"That doesn't make us wrong," Red Scar said.

"That is true," Quirk said. "Let me ask you something, Scar. How did you come by such a name? I've always been curious about the name, as I see no visible scars on you."

"I was born with this," Red Scar said and stood up. He moved the vest covering his chest and stood close to the fire to show Quirk the red birthmark in the shape of a leaf on his lower left abdomen.

"I suppose your parents could have named you Red Leaf," Quirk said.

Red Scar grinned and sat down. "What does the name Quirk mean?"

"I'm American," Quirk said. "Our names don't mean nothing of consequence."

"Neither does the word of the chiefs in Washington," Red Scar said.

"And that, my good friend, is the truth," Quirk said.

"Michele, are you asleep?" Michael whispered.

"No."

"Are they?"

"Looks like it."

"Something I have to tell you."

"What?"

"When Frog tied my hands I spread my wrists apart," Michael whispered. "In the dark he didn't see the ropes were loose."

"What are you saying, Mickey?"

"My hands are free," Michael whispered.

"What?"

"Be quiet while I untie my legs," Michael said. "Then I'll untie you, and we'll run for it."

"To where?" Michele asked.

"Anywhere."

"That's better than here I guess," Michele said.

# Twenty-Four

While Quirk was saddling his horse and checking his supplies, he didn't notice Red Scar walking up behind him with his horse in tow and his rifle in his left hand.

Quirk turned and looked at Red Scar.

"Going somewhere?" Quirk said.

"With you," Red Scar said.

"I told you this is a guerrilla operation," Quirk said.

"Your chiefs taught you about what you called guerrilla warfare," Red Scar said. "But they learned it from us a hundred and fifty years ago. Remember Custer? He was also a guerrilla fighter. I will ride with you."

Quirk nodded. "But if you get your fool head shot off, don't cry to me about it."

Red Scar placed his rifle into the sleeve on his saddle and mounted his horse.

Quirk looked at Red Scar and then, in one quick and graceful motion that didn't hurt his ribs all that much, he mounted his horse.

Together they rode out of camp, leaving the dog soldiers and the herd behind.

Miller held the ropes left behind by the twins in his left hand as he looked at Frog. With his right hand Miller drew his .44 revolver and smacked it against Frog's jaw.

"I told you tight!" Miller screamed as Frog fell in a heap.

"Come on, Frank, no call for that," Deeds said. "It ain't Frog's fault."

Miller holstered his gun and looked down at Frog.

"Get up," Miller snarled. "We have to waste half a day looking for those kids and you'll ride, busted jaw or not."

"They went north," Deeds said, looking at the tracks.

"Then so do we," Miller said. He looked at Frog. "You best hope nothing happened to them, or I'll give you the like in return."

They walked through the night. At sunrise Michael and Michael took a brief rest to drink water from the canteen Michael took off one of the horses.

"How far do you think we walked?" Michele asked.

"I don't know. Maybe five or six miles."

"That's not enough. They'll catch us for sure on horseback."

"I know they'll catch us. We have to give Mr. Quirk time to catch up to them. I don't believe he's dead."

"But what if he is?"

"We still have to try anyway."

"Maybe we can find a good place to hide?"

"I have an idea," Michael said. "They'll have to track us, right? Follow our footsteps? Right?"

"Right."

"Let's split up for a while. We'll walk in a half circle and then meet up. When they get to this point, they'll see two sets of tracks and they'll have to split up, too. That should give us some time to find a place to hide."

"Okay, but we'll keep each other in sight."

"Take this in case you get thirsty," Michael said and gave Michele the canteen. "But don't drink any unless you have to."

★ ★ ★ ★ ★

Quirk and Red Scar rode hard for several hours until they were sure they'd picked up Miller's trail.

They dismounted to inspect the deep tracks left behind by Miller and the others.

"Definitely moving southwest to Silver Springs," Quirk said.

"This horse is smaller," Red Scar said.

"It's the boy's," Quirk said. "Used to belong to my cook. He and his sister are probably riding together."

"The boy and girl are probably slowing them down," Red Scar said. "We can catch them in three days' time."

"Not if we stand around here talking about it we won't," Quirk said.

Kneeling, Deeds inspected the tracks and markings the twins had left in the grass and soft dirt.

"Looks like they split up right about here, Frank," Deeds said.

"Then so do we," Miller said. "Frog, you go with me."

Deeds mounted his horse. "I think it might be a trick, Frank," he said. "To split us up while they meet up down the road."

"When we catch them, I'll give them a trick they won't soon forget," Miller said. "Whoever finds them first fires a shot. Move out."

Michael and Michele stopped to rest under the shade of a tall poplar tree. They didn't know where they were, but they knew they were off the open range because the terrain wasn't as flat, and trees dotted the landscape.

"How far do you think we've gone?" Michele asked.

"I don't know. Far," Michael said. "But not far enough."

Michele took a sip of water. "I'm hungry, Michael."

"Me, too," Michael said. "I got these."

Michael removed several sticks of jerky from his shirt pocket and gave one to Michele. "We'll each have one now and save the others for later."

They munched on the jerky sticks and took several small sips of water.

"Michael, I'm really tired," Michele said.

"I know, but we can't stop until dark," Michael said. "They can't track us in the dark, and then we can rest."

"Michael, what's that?" Michele said.

Michael looked at the dots on the horizon. After a few seconds he saw tiny clouds of dust around the dots. The dots grew larger. The clouds of dust swirled around them.

"Mikey?"

"What?"

"Run."

Michael jumped up and grabbed Michele's arm and they took off running as fast as they could.

They ran maybe three hundred yards when they heard the thunder of horses behind them.

They continued to run, but they were tiring and losing speed.

The horses grew closer and closer.

And then a rope suddenly looped around Michael's chest, and he went flying to the ground.

"Michael!" Michele screamed.

Michael looked up. Miller held the other end of the rope, and he wrapped it around the saddle horn.

"I warned you not to run, didn't I?" Miller said and dragged Michael along the ground.

Michele ran after Michael, but Frog was off his horse and he grabbed her.

Miller dragged Michael thirty or forty feet, and then Frog said, "Frank, that's enough. He's just a boy, for God's sake."

Miller released the rope. He pulled his gun from the holster and fired one shot into the air to signal the others he'd found them.

"Let's go," Miller said to Frog. "They ride with you."

An hour before sunset Houle and Ferris rode into what was once the small, but prosperous, town of Silver Springs. Created by the railroad after the war, Silver Springs was to be a destination stop on the trip west. While the tracks were under construction, the town served as a supply depot.

When a land surveyor discovered a quicker, less expensive route to link the Atlantic to the Pacific, the town was abandoned and relocated twenty miles to the north under a new name.

As they rode down Main Street, Houle and Ferris took stock of the town. Tumbleweeds blew across the street and littered the rotting wood sidewalks. Shops and stores were deserted, with broken signs and busted windows.

The three-story hotel, once the crown jewel of the town, was now a rotting eyesore of a building, but a quick once-over told them the basic structure was still intact and safe to enter.

They dismounted in front of the hotel and tied their horses to what was left of the hitching post in the street.

"Let's check out the hotel and then the livery," Ferris said. "Maybe we can find something we can use."

Quirk and Red Scar rode for several hours after dark before finally making camp for the night.

Around a fire they ate a quick meal and drank coffee.

"If we push hard, we can make Silver Springs in less than two days," Quirk said.

Red Scar stuffed his pipe with tobacco and lit it with a stick from the fire.

"These kids mean a lot to you, don't they?" Red Scar said.

Quirk nodded as he filled his pipe. "It didn't start out that way," he said. "But I like to think that had mine lived and I had me another, they would have grown up like those two. Real smart and not afraid. I've seen kids raised in the city before. They're afraid of their own shadows. Not these two. The girl has the guts of a bank robber. That boy will grow up to be a fine man. They will grow up to be the kind of people who will make a difference in this country."

Red Scar puffed on his pipe and sipped some coffee.

"If they are allowed to grow up," Quirk said.

Quirk fished a stick out of the fire and lit his pipe.

"Why are you along on this?" Quirk said.

"I enjoy killing white men," Red Scar said.

"Don't give me that horse crap," Quirk said. "If that were true, you and your dog soldiers would have killed me off years ago."

Red Scar looked at Quirk and a sudden sadness came to his eyes.

"The year of the great uprising, my wife was but twenty-two years old. Our son was but three," Red Scar said. "The army came in great numbers to pacify us and put us on reservations. I rode with the Sioux during the uprising and when we were defeated and I returned to my wife and son, they were in the ground. I never found out why or who murdered them. Soldiers or a raid on our camp by a warring tribe looking to take advantage. I feel much like you do, that somebody has to pay for what they did, but I don't know who that somebody is and I probably never will."

Quirk stared into the campfire for a moment, and then looked at his friend.

"So, as you said, not these kids, not this time," Red Scar said.

"It's hard, isn't it?" Quirk said. "To keep going on when there's nothing left in your heart to go on for."

Red Scar nodded. "Yes."

"Something I've been meaning to do and now seems like the right time," Quirk said. He pulled the knife from its sheath on the left side of his gun belt. With the tip of the knife, he made a thin line on the left palm of his hand. When blood appeared, he held it to Red Scar.

Red Scar nodded, drew his knife, and made a similar cut on his left palm. Then they pressed hands together until their blood mingled as one.

"Blood or no blood, I still don't like sleeping in a bed," Red Scar said.

"Tell you the truth," Quirk said with a grin. "I don't either."

Frog washed Michael's face with a wet cloth. The boy had cuts and bruises from being dragged by Miller's horse. His left shoulder was probably dislocated. He had a slight fever and moaned softly in his sleep.

"My brother didn't deserve that," Michele said.

Frog looked at the girl, hog-tied against a saddle like some piglet.

"No, no he didn't," Frog said, softly.

★ ★ ★ ★ ★

# The Showdown

★ ★ ★ ★ ★

# TWENTY-FIVE

"Frank, the boy can't ride with that shoulder," Frog said.

"What's wrong with it?" Miller said.

"I think it's dislocated from when you dragged him."

"We'll be in Silver Springs by nightfall," Miller said. "Do something about it then."

"I don't think it can wait," Frog said. "The boy's passed out cold, and he's getting a fever. Do you want to deal with that now or later when he's worse?"

"Fix it then," Miller said. "Pep, you wait here and ride when the boy is able, but make it quick. Deeds, you ride with me. And Frog, you better catch up before dark."

Red Scar inspected the tracks in the soft grass and loose dirt.

"No more than a day and a half ahead of us," he said. "If that."

"Then the kids are doing their best to slow them down," Quirk said.

Red Scar stood up and patted his horse's neck.

"The horses are tired," he said. "They need rest and grain."

"All right," Quirk said. "You tend the horses. I'll gather some wood for a fire."

"Hold him still around the chest," Frog told Pep. "Whatever you do, don't let him turn away. I want to set his shoulder, not break it."

Unconscious, Michael was a dead weight in Pep's arms.

"What are you gonna do?" Pep asked.

"Try and set the boy's shoulder back in place so he can ride."

Frog took hold of Michael by the left arm. Michael moaned without opening his eyes. Gently Frog lifted Michael's arm so that it was level with his shoulder.

"Twist to the left when I say three," Frog said.

"My left or yours?"

"The boy's left," Frog said. "One . . . two . . . three."

Pep twisted Michael to the left as Frog yanked down and hard on the shoulder. There was a loud pop and Michael screamed without waking up. The shoulder snapped back into place.

"Let him go," Frog said.

Pep released Michael, and the boy fell into Frog's arms.

"We'll let him sleep for a bit and then we'll catch up with Frank," Frog said.

"I need a drink," Pep said. "I got me a pint in my saddlebags."

"Pour a spoon down the boy's throat," Frog said. "Help ease the pain a bit when he wakes up."

Brushing their horses side-by-side, Quirk looked at the Winchester rifle resting against Red Scar's saddle.

"What year model is your Winchester?" Quirk said.

" 'Seventy-three, but I didn't get it until 'seventy-five," Red Scar said.

"It's a fine rifle," Quirk said. "Why don't you have a sidearm?"

"I never had much use for one," Red Scar said.

"I have three extra sidearms in my saddlebags," Quirk said. "One is mine I use as a spare, two belonged to the bushwhackers I killed when they snuck into camp at night. They're not new, but in fine working order. Why don't you take one of them? The Colt."

"I'll stick with the Winchester," Red Scar said. "It's never failed me."

"I agree that it's a fine weapon, but a Colt makes a good backup in an emergency," Quirk said. "Besides that, we might find us in a situation where a rifle won't do. Why don't you take the Colt, Scar? I'd feel better if you carried it."

Red Scar looked at Quirk. "I haven't fired a revolver in a dozen years."

Quirk opened his saddlebags and removed the Colt revolver he used as a spare. It was wrapped in cloth. He removed the cloth and held it to Red Scar.

"Cost thirty-five dollars new a few years ago," Quirk said. "Has a real nice balance and is as accurate as a Winchester up to seventy-five feet. I'm making it a gift to you for you to keep as your own."

Red Scar took the blued revolver by its black ivory handle and felt the perfect balance in his hand.

"Get the feel of it," Quirk said. "Fire off a few shots at that poplar over there."

Red Scar looked at the tree some twenty yards away.

He cocked the Colt, aimed, fired, and missed the tree by yards. He fired two more shots that also missed the tree by yards.

"Maybe the sight got bent," Quirk said. "Let me try."

Red Scar passed the Colt to Quirk. He cocked and fired three shots into the poplar in a small, tight group.

"Maybe if you practiced a bit?" Quirk said as he opened the chamber to empty the spent shells and reload.

"It isn't the Colt," Red Scar said. He picked up his Winchester, cocked the lever and aimed at a poplar a hundred or more yards away, and fired a shot dead center.

Quirk looked at Red Scar.

"What is it then?" Quirk asked.

Red Scar set the Winchester against his saddle. He opened a saddlebag, removed something, and kept his back to Quirk so he couldn't see.

"Tell one man living or dead, and I will take your scalp," Red Scar said and turned to Quirk.

Quirk stared at the rimless eyeglasses perched on Red Scar's broad nose.

"You're kidding me?" Quirk said. "Spectacles?"

"Things get a little fuzzy up close," Red Scar said. "The doctor in Denver said it was normal for a man of my age. He gave me these for looking at things close. Otherwise, he said I squint, and that throws off my aim at short distances."

Quirk burst out laughing. "You look like Ben Franklin," he said as he caught his breath.

"You giggle like an old woman. Shut up and give me the Colt," Red Scar said and yanked the revolver from Quirk's grasp.

Rapid-firing the Colt, Red Scar hit the tree six out of six shots. He lowered the weapon to his side and nodded. "You're right," he said. "It has a real nice balance."

With Michael on the front of his saddle, Frog rode into Miller's campsite with Pep right behind him.

"Michael, are you all right?" asked Michele, her legs tied with rope.

"He's okay," Frog said as he dismounted and helped Michael from the saddle. "Just tired and in some pain. He'll be fine by tomorrow, although he'll hurt some."

Miller stood over Michael and stared down at the boy.

"I warned you, didn't I?" Miller said. "Now go sit over there by your sister and keep your mouth shut."

"Houle and Ferris come back?" Pep said as he dismounted.

"No," Miller said. "So we ride into Silver Springs in the morning as planned."

"How long you figure to be gone?" Frog said.

"Not long," Miller said. "A few days at most. We'll have to stay in the ghost town for a while, so I'll bring back extra supplies."

"Is there any chance she won't pay?" Deeds asked.

"She'll pay," Miller said. "These brats are her heirs, and she has millions to spare. Give the boy some chow and make sure they can't run away again. We'll leave at first light."

Late in the afternoon, Quirk and Red Scar rode into the campsite left behind by Miller earlier in the morning.

Red Scar shuffled the abandoned remains of a fire and stirred the ashes with a stick to pick up the scent.

"Ten hours ahead of us at most," he said.

"They reached Silver Springs by now," Quirk said.

Red Scar checked the tracks leading away from the campsite.

"The boy's horse is still with them," he said.

"No doubt the girl, too," Quirk said. "Miller wants his full amount of bloodsucker money before he's done with them."

"Do you want to ride or camp?" Red Scar said.

"Our horses need rest," Quirk said. "Us, too, and they're not going anywhere just yet."

"I'll gather up some wood."

Houle and Ferris were sitting on the steps of the hotel when Miller and the group rode into town along Main Street.

With nothing much to do for a day and a half, Houle and Ferris explored each building in the deserted town. While most residents took everything with them they could carry when they vacated, some useful things were left behind.

A storage room in the hotel basement was filled with mattresses, linen, and blankets, enough for all of them to have a warm bed. A storage chest in the dining room was stacked with dishes and silverware. One of three dry goods stores had some canned goods and fruit in a back room.

One table with six chairs remained in the hotel dining room.

Under the bar in one of the saloons they found a sealed bottle of brandy, which they sipped on the steps of the hotel as Miller and the boys rode toward the hotel.

Houle stood up from the steps.

"Wondering when you was going to get here," he said.

Miller dismounted at the steps.

"Had some trouble with the brats," he said. "How are things here?"

"Quiet as a church on a Tuesday night," Ferris said.

"We got things fixed up real nice at the hotel," Houle said "Even the old cooking stove in the kitchen still works."

"Good," Miller said. "First thing in the morning, I'll ride over to Medicine Bow and send that wire to Chicago. What are you drinking there, Ferris?"

"Brandy. It's decent. Want a snort?"

"I could use one," Miller said.

Quirk and Red Scar leaned against their saddles and sipped coffee laced with a splash of whiskey. Each smoked their pipe, and the air around the campfire was sweet with the aroma of grass and tobacco.

"How many men are we after?" Red Scar said.

"A total of six."

"We will have to kill them all to rescue the boy and girl."

"I know."

"You have killed many," Red Scar said.

"During the war and after," Quirk said. "But I never murdered anybody or killed anybody that wasn't trying to kill or rob me or do someone harm."

"I have killed many numbers as well," Red Scar said. "Many

Sioux, Apache, Crow, and Blackfeet before the whites came in numbers, and then I killed many whites after that. When I was a young warrior, it never occurred to me that a man could grow tired of killing, but I have."

Quirk took a sip from his cup. "Hell, Scar, it's easy to kill," he said. "Learning how to live with others is the hard part. Harder still when everything you love is taken away from you."

Red Scar sipped from his cup and then nodded.

"I haven't killed a white man in many years," he said. "But I will enjoy killing these white men."

"As long as the boy and girl aren't harmed in the process, I don't care if you skin and roast them on a spit," Quirk said.

"I'd rather eat rotten government beef," Red Scar said.

Miller inspected the empty bedroom where a mattress, sheets, and blanket had been set up the day before.

"Got some candles by the mattress," Houle said. "Found a box of 'em in the kitchen."

"What about the brats?" Miller said. "I want them in the same room with one of the men in there at all times."

Houle nodded. "Want some grub? We fired up the old wood oven in the kitchen."

"Make it quick. I want to get some sleep," Miller said. "And tell Frog I want to see him right away."

Houle left the second-floor room and closed the door. Miller sat on the mattress, rolled a cigarette, and struck a wood match on the floor to light it.

Frog knocked on the door, opened it, and stepped inside.

"You want to see me, Frank?"

"Close the door."

Frog shut the door.

"Something wrong, Frank?"

"I need you to make the trip to Medicine Bow with me in

the morning. We could be holed up in the town for a few weeks, maybe even three. We need supplies. I could buy a mule to haul supplies, but I don't want to cause any attention or give someone a reason to remember my face. If we both buy supplies at two different stores, we can haul enough back to last us a while. If we run out, two of the boys can make the trip and do the same thing."

"You think we'll be here that long?"

"Three weeks at least," Miller said. "Two million in bonds is no small transaction, and then to send them by train to Medicine Bow, it could be that long or longer."

"All right, Frank. We'll head out right after breakfast."

"Hey, Scar?" Quirk said.

Red Scar rolled over in his bedroll and looked at Quirk.

"You can kill all the others if you want to, but Miller is mine," Quirk said. "Nobody touches that miserable bushwhacker but me."

Red Scar nodded, rolled back over, and closed his eyes.

Quirk stared at the stars overhead. It was a clear night, and there were too many to count even if he was so inclined.

"Yes, sir. Nobody touches that miserable bushwhacker but me," Quirk whispered to himself and closed his eyes.

# Twenty-Six

"We should be back inside of three days' ride," Miller said. "Keep the brats locked up and make sure that nothing happens to them while we're away. I'm holding you men responsible if anything happens while we're gone."

"Hey, Frog, we could use some sipping whiskey," Ferris said. "Rye if they got it. Anything if they don't."

"I'll bring a bottle," Frog said.

Miller and Frog mounted their horses and rode down Main Street and out of Silver Springs.

In front of the hotel, Ferris watched them go. When they were gone, he walked up the steps and entered the hotel.

From a room on the second floor, Deeds watched Miller and Frog ride out of town. He turned away from the window and looked at Michael and Michele, who were seated on a mattress in the corner.

"There they go," Deeds said.

"How long do we have to stay here?" Michele asked.

"As long as it takes," Deeds said.

"And then what happens?" Michael asked.

"You go home," Deeds said. "And we get rich."

"Back to Chicago?" Michele said.

"That's where you're from, ain't it?" Deeds said.

"But it's not where we were going," Michael said.

"San Francisco, that's right," Deeds said. "Well, you'll just have to settle for Chicago and be thankful for that."

"Can we get up and walk around?" Michele said. "All this sitting hurts my back."

"I suppose it won't hurt none," Deeds said. "Let me get ahold of Pep and we'll go downstairs for a bit and get some air."

After a quick breakfast at dawn, Quirk and Red Scar rode hard for most of the day. They stopped just once to rest the horses and eat a lunch of jerky and water. Otherwise, they road fast without talking or slowing their speed.

By late afternoon they dismounted and stood in a field just a half mile from Silver Springs.

Quirk dug his binoculars out of a saddlebag and scanned the ghost town.

"Doesn't look like much," he said. "We'll do some reconnaissance after dark."

Red Scar took the binoculars and looked at the deserted buildings and streets of the town.

"You're right, it doesn't look like much," Red Scar said.

"My guess is they made themselves comfortable in that old hotel and are using the livery for the horses. We'll know for sure in a few hours when we go in."

Red Scar and Quirk removed the saddles from their horses, and gave them grain and a good brushing to rid their coats of salt.

"We'll walk into town from a side street," Quirk said. "It's the only way to know for sure where they are."

Red Scar tossed his bedroll onto the ground.

"We have time for a few hours sleep," he said.

Quirk grabbed his bedroll. "And I sure could use it."

★ ★ ★ ★ ★

Hours after dark, Quirk and Red Scar entered Silver Springs from the west side of the town. The moon was bright, and they traveled easily along the streets by its light. They walked in the dirt streets, avoiding the rotted, creaky wood sidewalks.

Tumbleweeds rolled by them on a soft night breeze.

Silver Springs consisted of five block-long streets and about twenty buildings in all. Some of the buildings were never completed, as once the railroad selected a new location for its stop, construction was halted.

The livery stables were located on the fifth street facing south.

Quirk and Red Scar quietly entered the livery where five horses were tethered in open stalls.

"That's the boy's horse in the second stall," Quirk said.

"Two are missing," Red Scar said.

"Either they didn't arrive yet, or Miller took a man with him to Medicine Bow for supplies and to send a wire to Chicago," Quirk said. "Come on."

The only sign of life in the town came from the hotel. Once the crown jewel of Silver Springs, the broken-down three-story structure sat in the center of Main Street.

Light shone from four separate rooms on the second floor.

"They must have the boy and girl in the hotel with them," Red Scar said.

"And there isn't a whole lot we can do about it right now," Quirk said. "Come on, I've seen enough."

They camped a mile from the town on the south side of Silver Springs where their campfire wouldn't be seen from the hotel.

Quirk used a stick to draw the town in the dirt by the fire and outlined his plan.

"We have to move fast and strike quickly," Quirk said. "There is no second chance. As much as you don't want to, you'll need to wear them eyeglasses."

Red Scar nodded.

"Surprise will equalize the numbers, so don't worry about the odds being in their favor," Quirk said. "They'll be overconfident in their numbers, anyway. The important thing is to kill them quick, so the boy and his sister aren't harmed. Otherwise we're doing this for nothing."

Red Scar studied Quirk's scratching in the dirt.

"We have to move out in four hours," Quirk said. "Do you want to sleep or pass the time with some coffee and sipping whiskey?"

Stuffing his pipe with tobacco, Red Scar looked at Quirk.

"Do you need to ask?" Red Scar said.

# Twenty-Seven

An hour before the sun came up, Quirk stood watch in the street while Red Scar entered the livery stables.

Red Scar was inside the stables for about fifteen minutes. When he came out he had five horses saddled and held in tow with a rope.

"Take them out a few hundred yards and hobble them," Quirk said. "I'll keep an eye out from here."

While Red Scar led the horses out to the field behind the livery, Quirk gathered up some large balls of dry tumbleweed and tossed them into the empty stalls of the stable. He pulled his thin flask from a back pocket and splashed whiskey onto the tumbleweeds and dry walls, then walked outside to wait for Red Scar to return.

Red Scar was gone about twenty minutes. While he waited, Quirk stuffed and lit his pipe.

Finally Red Scar emerged from the darkness and stood behind Quirk.

"Sun will be up shortly," Quirk said. "Want a stick of jerky?"

"Our final meal?" Red Scar said as he took a stick.

They munched on the jerky while they waited for the sun to rise. As it slowly lightened the streets, Quirk nodded to Red Scar that it was time.

"Put your man down with the first shot," Quirk said. "We will have surprise as an advantage, but that will only last for a short while, so that first shot has to count. After you take out the first man, move onto the next. They will panic for a few seconds, but then recover and look for shelter. We can't let that happen. Are you ready?"

"I was ready before you started talking," Red Scar said as he slipped on his glasses.

Quirk looked at the glasses perched on Red Scar's nose and grinned. "You're a fine sight in the morning, you know that," he said.

"Without them I might shoot you, and we don't want that," Red Scar said.

"No," Quirk said. "We don't."

"Do it if you're going to do it," Red Scar said.

Quirk entered the livery, removed a match from his shirt pocket, touched it to the bowl of his pipe, and then tossed it onto the tumbleweed. The dry weed immediately burst into flames and quickly spread across the rotted wood.

Quirk went outside, joined Red Scar, and together they walked out of town.

Deeds was awake on his mattress, smoking a rolled cigarette and watching the twins on their mattress when he suddenly caught the scent of something from the street.

The twins, tied together at the ankles and waist, smelled it too and they struggled to sit up.

"I smell something," Michael said.

"Quiet," Deeds said as he got up and went to the open window.

He stuck his head out and looked up and down the empty street. Then he saw it. Smoke billowing on the breeze coming from the west side of the town.

"Fire," Deeds said.

★ ★ ★ ★ ★

Deeds, Pep, Houle, and Ferris came out of the hotel and searched for what was burning.

"The livery," Deeds said. "The horses."

They ran down the alleyway beside the hotel to the edge of town where the livery was engulfed in flames.

"I don't see them," Deeds said. "They must have gotten out somehow."

"To where?" Pep said.

From the east end of the street, Quirk appeared on horseback, his massive Colt revolver cocked and ready.

From the west end of the street, Red Scar appeared on horseback, his Colt held high in the air.

Without hesitation, Quirk charged.

Then Red Scar charged.

Deeds and Pep looked west.

Houle and Ferris looked east.

Quirk shot Deeds in the heart from thirty feet before the man even knew what was happening.

In a panic, Pep reached for his gun, but Quirk cocked his Colt and shot Pep in the chest from twenty feet. The man fell dead.

Charging Houle and Ferris, Red Scar fired, missed the first shot, cocked and fired again, and hit Houle in the neck. The few seconds' delay gave Ferris time to pull his gun and fire at Red Scar. The bullet grazed Red Scar's right shoulder, knocking him off his horse.

Quirk stopped his horse and turned around in time to see Red Scar hit the ground. He raced to Red Scar, who bounced up to his feet.

"I'm all right!" Red Scar shouted. "He's getting away!"

Quirk turned and saw Ferris disappear down the alley. He cocked the Colt, yanked the reins, and steered his horse to the alleyway. He emerged on the street ready to shoot.

But Ferris was nowhere in sight.

A moment later, Red Scar, mounted again, appeared next to Quirk.

"The hotel," Quirk said.

They raced their horses to Main Street, turned, and trotted to the hotel.

Quirk looked up at the windows. Several were open.

"You in the hotel, I'll give you one chance to surrender!" Quirk yelled. "Your friends are dead! You're alone now! I see no sense in you dying for no reason when you don't have to!"

From a window on the second floor, Ferris shouted, "No good, Quirk. I don't trust you one bit!"

"All I want are the kids!" Quirk said. "Give me them, and you walk away alive."

"Too thin for me, Quirk!" Ferris said. "Like I said, I don't trust you! Now you and that savage ride out of town. When I see you on the horizon, I'll set the kids free. Otherwise I'll kill them right here in this room!"

"How do I know you won't kill them the moment we ride out?" Quirk said.

"You don't," Ferris shouted. "But that's the only deal you'll get from me. Where is my horse?"

"Not far behind the livery," Quirk said.

"You get my horse and leave him out front here. He's got a white diamond on his nose," Ferris said. "When I see you two in the distance, I'll ride out west in the opposite direction. When I'm clear, I'll fire a shot and you come get these kids."

"I want your word you won't harm those kids," Quirk said.

"All you got is five minutes to get my horse and ride out," Ferris said. "Starting now."

"I'll need more than five minutes," Quirk said.

"Well, that's all you got," Ferris said. "I'm no murderer, but you need to know I won't go to Yuma for Frank Miller, and I'll do what I have to do not to. Now ride."

"All right," Quirk said.

Quirk and Red Scar rode down the alley to the burning livery and past it to the open field where the horses were hobbled and eating grass.

Quirk dismounted and removed the leather straps from the horse with the white diamond on his nose.

"You know what he's going to do, don't you?" Red Scar said.

"Yeah," Quirk said. "He's going to take one or both of them as a hostage so we don't follow him."

"We can always track him and—"

"No." Quirk took the reins of the white horse, mounted his own horse, and said, "Come on, I have an idea."

Ferris looked out the window of the hotel room and watched the street.

"This is taking too long," he said.

From the mattress, Michael said, "I told you Mr. Quirk would come for us."

"Shut your mouth or I'll shut it for you," Ferris said.

"You're scared," Michael said. "I can see it on your face."

"I told you to shut up," Ferris snapped. "And I won't tell you again."

Down below, Red Scar appeared with his horse. Ferris said, "Where's Quirk?"

"In the field where you told him to go," Red Scar said.

"Where? I don't see him," Ferris said.

"Give us a moment," Red Scar said.

Red Scar turned and rode out of town. From the window, Ferris couldn't see him until suddenly he joined up with Quirk, and they rode east.

"I'll give them five more minutes to get far enough away," Ferris said.

Michael and Michele exchanged glances.

"Mr. Quirk left us?" Michele said.

"He had to, girl," Ferris said. "To save your life. You should be thankful that he did what he did."

Quirk moved quickly along Main Street, staying close to the buildings so that Ferris couldn't see him from the window. He reached the hotel, removed the Peacemaker from its holster, cocked it, and raced into the lobby.

Quirk ran up the steps to the second floor, kicked in the door to the room where Ferris looked out the window, and when Ferris turned and attempted to draw his gun, Quirk shot him in the chest. Ferris toppled over backward and spilled out the window.

Quirk went to the window and fired two shots to signal Red Scar, turned, and looked at the twins.

"You hurt?" Quirk asked.

"No, sir," Michael said.

Quirk holstered the Peacemaker and drew his knife. He bent down to cut the ropes. As soon as Michele was free, she grabbed Quirk's neck and hugged him so tightly, Quirk could hardly breathe.

"They said you were dead, but I knew you weren't," Michele said. "I just knew you weren't."

Quirk lifted her in his arms. "It was touch and go there for a while, but here I am," he said.

"Can we get out of here now?" Michael said.

At the two shots Quirk fired out the window, Red Scar stopped his horse and looked at the body of Deeds tied to one of the remaining horses. Quirk's hat was perched on Deeds's head.

Red Scar grabbed the hat, turned the horses around, and rode back into town.

For the first time in many years, Red Scar ate a meal at a table off dishes in a hotel dining room.

"When did Miller leave?" Quirk asked the twins.

"Yesterday morning," Michael said.

Quirk looked at Red Scar.

"I will protect them like they were my own," Red Scar said.

Michael looked at Red Scar. "What do you mean?"

Michele looked at Quirk. "What does he mean, Mr. Quirk?"

"He's going after Miller," Red Scar said. "It's the only way."

"You're leaving us?" Michele said. "You can't do that."

"I have to," Quirk said. "There's no telling what a man like Frank Miller will do when cornered. If I don't stop him now, he'll come back to haunt you later one way or another. Men like Miller have a funny way about revenge, even when they're in the wrong."

Michele turned away to wipe her eyes.

Quirk looked at Michael. "Take one of the bigger horses and give your sister the small one," he said.

"Yes, sir," Michael said.

Quirk stood up from the table

"Scar, meet up with the herd," Quirk said. "If I'm not back inside a week, you and the kids here take my herd to Omaha to the army fort. Keep the money for your tribe. My way of saying thanks."

Red Scar nodded.

Quirk walked out of the dining room.

Michele stood up from the table.

Red Scar pointed a finger at her.

"No," Red Scar said. "He wants you to stay here."

# Twenty-Eight

"Are you ready?" Red Scar asked.

Atop Michael's horse, Michele nodded.

Riding the horse that belonged to Deeds, Michael said, "Yes, sir."

With the remaining horses in tow, loaded down with supplies and water, Red Scar nodded and led the way out of town.

No one was particularly hungry, so they skipped lunch and rode until nearly sunset, a total of almost fifteen miles.

In front of a campfire as they ate supper, Michele said, "Mr. Red Scar, what did Mr. Quirk mean when he said Mr. Miller will come back to haunt us?"

Loading his pipe with tobacco, Red Scar looked at Michele.

"Frank Miller is a man possessed by greed," Red Scar said. "When he finds out his plan went bad and he's wanted by the law, there is no telling what he'll do to get even. Out of spite, he might try to kill you and your aunt in Chicago."

"But Mr. Quirk is alone," Michele said.

"Quirk is a guerrilla fighter," Red Scar said. "And from what I know of him, a damned good one."

Quirk rode through the day, munching on jerky sticks in the saddle. He stopped only once for two hours to rest and feed his horse.

He gave the horse grain and sugar cubes and a good brushing, and then rode on through the night until morning. He kept the horse at a steady pace so he wouldn't tire and dismounted at sunrise for a two-hour rest.

He rested long enough to fix a hot breakfast and feed and brush his horse again.

"I'm asking for a lot, I know," he said as he brushed his horse's back. "But if we make it out of this alive and get back to the ranch, I'll retire you to pasture where all you have to worry about is which patch of grass is the sweetest and which filly catches your fancy."

"Two, plus a half day's ride, and we should reach the herd," Red Scar said.

Michael added some wood to the campfire. "I won't leave Mr. Quirk," he said. "You can go to Omaha if you want to, but I won't go."

"I won't either," Michele said.

"You heard what Quirk said," Red Scar said.

"I don't care," Michele said. "I won't go. You'll have to tie me up and force me."

Red Scar looked at Michael. "You feel the same?"

Michael nodded.

"Good," Red Scar said. "Then we all agree on what we should do."

Two hours after sunrise, Quirk spotted two dots coming his way on the horizon. He was brushing his horse when he first noticed them. There was plenty of time, so he continued brushing his horse and then gave him a few cubes of sugar.

Then Quirk carefully saddled his horse. He checked the Peacemaker to make sure it was fully loaded, then grabbed a spare revolver from the saddlebags and did the same before tucking it into his belt.

Looking at the dots grow larger on the horizon, Quirk

mounted his horse.

Quirk rubbed his horse's neck to keep him calm.

"We had this poem in the army during the war, you see," he said. "I don't remember all of it, but enough."

Quirk pulled the Colt, cocked it and held it in his right hand, yanked the reins, and his horse took off running.

"Half a league, half a league, half a league onward," Quirk said aloud, as if to give courage to his horse.

Quirk raced his horse directly into the path of Miller and Frog.

"Frog, do you see what I see?" Miller said.

"Yup," Frog said. "Quirk."

"He's alive."

"Sure looks that way."

"I don't believe it," Miller said.

"Believe it, Frank," Frog said. "That Peacemaker in his hand means business."

When a hundred feet separated the charging Quirk from a charging Miller and Frog, Quirk fired the first shot.

Miller fired the second.

Both shots missed their targets.

Quirk charged closer and fired two more shots. One struck Miller in the left side of his chest. The other shot hit him in the left shoulder.

Miller fell from his horse.

Unable to stop his horse, Frog's horse panicked, jumped over Miller, and Frog went flying to the ground.

Quirk saw it a moment too late. His horse, spooked by having to leap over Frog's body, tossed Quirk to the ground and accidently struck Quirk in the head with his left leg.

Miller slowly rose from the ground. He looked for his gun

and spotted it ten feet away. He walked over to pick it up.

Quirk, dazed from the blow delivered by his horse, tried to get up but fell to his knees and put his head down.

Miller cocked his gun as he walked to Quirk.

"You are one tough one cowboy, I'll give you that," Miller said.

Still on his knees, Quirk's head was starting to clear, and he looked around for his Colt. It was too far away to reach, so he tried to stand.

At that moment, Miller aimed his gun and shot Quirk in the right side of the abdomen.

"You put two holes in me, Quirk," Miller said. "I'm going to return the favor. That was one."

On his back now, Quirk looked at Miller.

Miller cocked his gun, aimed, and pulled the trigger.

The hammer made the metallic sound of striking a spent round. Miller opened the loading gate and started dumping the empties.

"Don't die just yet," Miller said. "Let me reload first."

Suddenly Frog was standing in front of Miller. His gun was in his right hand and hanging loosely by his side.

"I've done a lot of rotten things for you, Frank," Frog said. "But this ain't one of them."

Miller looked at Frog.

Frog cocked his gun and aimed it at Miller.

"No, wait," Miller said as Frog shot him dead.

Frog holstered his gun and looked at Quirk.

"How bad?" Frog said.

"Went right through," Quirk said.

"Let me have a look," Frog said.

Frog knelt beside Quirk and opened his shirt. The hole in the front side of Quirk's abdomen wasn't too bad, but the exit wound was larger and bleeding heavily.

"You know what I have to do?" Frog said.

"Yeah," Quirk said. "Best get to it before I bleed out."

Frog went to his saddlebags, dug out a quart bottle of rye whiskey, and gave it to Quirk.

"Take a few pulls on this while I make a fire," Frog said.

Quirk took the bottle, removed the cork, and took a long swallow.

Frog gathered up some sticks and tumbleweed into a pile. "Let me have the bottle," he said.

Quirk gave him the bottle, and Frog poured some whiskey onto the tumbleweed. He struck a match, tossed it onto the pile, and it immediately ignited.

Frog returned the bottle to Quirk and said, "Better have some more while I heat the knife."

Quirk took several more swallows from the bottle while Frog stuck his knife into the fire to the ivory handle.

"Let me know when you're ready," Frog said.

Quirk sipped whiskey and nodded.

Frog removed a bullet from his gun belt and looked at Quirk. "Let me have your knife."

Using Quirk's knife, Frog removed the bullet from its casing. "Ready?"

"Ready or not, it's got to be done or I'll bleed to death," Quirk said.

"We'll do the front first," Frog said. "That will get you prepared for the back."

Quirk took a final sip of whiskey and gave the bottle to Frog.

"You want something to bite on?" Frog said.

"Yeah, a thick, juicy steak."

"Fresh out," Frog grinned.

"Just my luck," Quirk said.

Frog poured some whiskey into the open wound in Quirk's abdomen and Quirk cringed. Frog pulled out a handkerchief from a pocket and dabbed the wound dry. Then he sprinkled some gunpowder on the hole.

"Grit hard," Frog said.

Quirk braced himself as Frog pulled the hot knife from the fire, placed it against the wound, and the gunpowder ignited and seared the flesh closed.

Quirk closed his eyes and swallowed the pain. His face was beaded in sweat, his arms and hands shook, the smell of his burning flesh was in his nose.

Frog returned the knife to the fire.

"Had . . . this done . . . once before," Quirk said. "By a sawbones in 'sixty-four when I took a Reb bullet to the leg. Still aches in wintertime right before it snows."

"I saw it done many times myself," Frog said. "I served with Grant."

"A fine general," Quirk said. "I was with Sherman. Ready for the backside."

"Best take a few more swallows first," Frog said and gave Quirk the whiskey bottle.

Quirk took several long gulps of whiskey. "Go on ahead and finish it," he said and rolled over.

Frog took the bottle, poured some on the wound, dabbed it dry, and sprinkled gunpowder on it.

"Get braced," Frog said. "Grit hard."

Quirk tightened his body, clenched his teeth, and Frog placed the knife against the wound. The powder ignited, flesh burned, Quirk ate the white-hot pain for as long as he could stand it and then passed out cold.

Quirk opened his eyes to a crackling fire and the smell of bacon and beans cooking in a fry pan.

He was in his bedroll.

The ache in his abdomen was brutal. He turned and looked

at Frog, who was kneeling and stirring the food with a wood spoon.

"How long I been out?" Quirk said.

"Long enough for me to bury Frank and fix up some grub," Frog said. "It's ready if you can sit up against your saddle."

Quirk tried to sit up, but it was like his sides were being ripped open.

"I'll give you a hand," Frog said.

With Frog's help, Quirk managed to sit up and brace his back against his saddle.

"Want some coffee?" Frog said.

"I could use a cup."

Frog filled two cups, added a shot of rye to each, gave one to Quirk, and then sat against his own saddle.

"I never thought any man could run down Frank Miller," Frog said. "I saw him do in four men in a Kansas City saloon once. The others?"

"Dead," Quirk said. "I had to do what I had to do to save the kids. The boy and his sister are being taken to my herd by Red Scar."

"The war chief? I've heard of him."

"He's a trusted friend of mine."

"That doesn't surprise me much."

"Why did you save me?" Quirk asked.

Frog sipped some coffee and looked at Quirk. "Frank was no good, I know that," he said. "After the war I went to work for his father as an agent. When the old man died and Frank took over, he wasn't like you saw him now. Something happened to him once he took control of the agency. Greed went to his head and guided his actions. I done some things I ain't proud of working for Frank, but this one was too much for me to swallow and still live with myself."

"I'm glad you came around to that thought when you did," Quirk said.

"Me too. Want some grub?"

Quirk looked up at the stars from his bedroll.

Beside him, Frog did the same.

"I have to catch up to them kids and the herd," Quirk said.

"Four or five days in the saddle is a hard ride for a man with your kind of bellyache," Frog said.

"I'll make do."

"We'll talk about it in the morning," Frog said.

"If I didn't say it already, thank you for saving my life," Quirk said.

"Least I could do, seeing as how I almost got you killed in the first place," Frog said.

# Twenty-Nine

Red Scar rode out a few hundred yards for a better look at the open plains. After three days, there was no sign of Quirk. He wasn't exactly worried, but his concern was growing with each passing day. He thought about backtracking, but if Quirk took a different route they would miss each other on the trail and maybe never meet up at all.

Around camp there was little to do except move the herd from one grazing point to another and play the game of stickball.

Red Scar's soldiers taught the game to Michael and Michele. A ball made of leather stuffed with cloth was moved along the ground with long sticks. The object was to take the ball from your opponent and score a point by hitting the ball against a pole made of wood and decorated with paint.

Since they didn't bring poles with them, the soldiers designated two trees as the goalposts.

The soldiers played the game hard. Cuts, bruises, and even broken bones were in order when an all-out match was played. Some tribes settled grudges with a match played to the death. When Michael and Michele were on the field, the soldiers tamped it down and allowed the twins to keep up with them.

Red Scar returned to the herd and watched the game for a while until Michael and Michele took a break.

"Tomorrow we move the herd to new grass," Red Scar said.

"Mr. Quirk shouldn't be much longer, should he?" Michele said. She was worried, but tried her best not to show it.

"A few more days," Red Scar said.

"What if he's hurt and needs help?" Michael said.

"Can't we go look for him?" Michele said.

"A few more days," Red Scar said.

"Best help me on my horse," Quirk said. "And I'll be on my way."

"You won't make a half day's ride before you fall out of the saddle," Frog said as he gave Quirk a boost onto his horse.

"I'll make it," Quirk said.

Frog removed leather strips from his saddlebags and said, "Give me your hands."

Quirk placed his hands on the saddle horn and Frog secured them in place with the leather strips.

Then Frog mounted his horse, took Quirk's horse by the reins, and, with Miller's horse acting as a pack mule in tow, Frog led the way east.

Michael and Michele walked with Red Scar through an open field of tall grass where the cattle and horses were quietly grazing.

Chicago seemed so long ago to the twins. Like some distant memory they couldn't quite visualize. Their aunt's wealth and the fine clothes and fancy school and carriages—it all seemed like a time from another life lived by a different set of twins.

Their clothes were tattered, their hands rough with dirty fingernails. They had learned to ride a horse out here. When they lived in Chicago, the closest they got to a horse was when they took a carriage ride and were allowed to pet it.

A soft bed would seem strange to them now. So would a fine table with linen and comfortable chairs.

They knew what waited for them in San Francisco. More of the same of what they'd had in Chicago.

A life of soft luxury.

Of soft sheets and rich food.

And clean fingernails.

Fine schools and mixing with the sons and daughters of others so privileged. It was living high, but it wasn't life. Even at their young age, they came to understand that the pleasure in life came from living it in a way that made you happy, and not the wealth that you possessed.

Red Scar paused to look in the distance. The grass was tall, the yellow wildflowers bloomed by the thousands, the air was sweet, the sky so blue it hurt their eyes to look at it.

"Mr. Red Scar," Michael said. "When Mr. Quirk arrives, do we have to go home?"

Frog looked back at Quirk. The cowboy was passed out in the saddle, held in place by the leather strips.

It looked like the cowboy might have a fever. Frog pulled out his pocket watch. Two hours to dark. He'd ride another hour and make camp for the night.

"You have a fever," Frog said. "High."

In his bedroll, Quirk nodded. "I figured as much."

"Nothing to do but sweat it out," Frog said. "Drink this coffee. It has whiskey in it to make you sweat."

Quirk sat up a bit and took the cup from Frog.

"I'll toss some extra blankets on you and build up the fire," Frog said. "Make you sweat a lot. You'll get the chills and your teeth will rattle, but it's the fastest way to sweat out a fever."

Quirk sipped from the cup. "It should be the other way around. This whiskey has some coffee in it."

Tossing wood onto the fire, Frog said, "Are you hungry? There's some birds on the spit."

"I ain't, but I'll eat one to keep my strength up," Quirk said.

He took another sip from the cup. "All the sawbones and their studying, you'd think they'd come up with something better than sweat for a fever."

*He was a young man working the fields of his farm in Indiana. His wife carried a pitcher of cold lemonade to him, and they sat in the shade of a giant oak tree to drink it. The war hadn't touched them yet, and it seemed as if their life together was a giant promise of good things to come.*

*But it did touch them, and he left Allison and their baby girl behind to go off and fight for what was theirs. For what they didn't want to lose.*

*And late in the war in February of 'sixty-five, he scouted a battlefield in Georgia with his men and came upon a small band of Rebel soldiers making camp. He begged them to surrender, but they would not. Instead they attacked, and his men were forced to put them down. Quirk killed the last of them, a Reb soldier with just his bayonet left for a weapon. His 1861 Navy Colt cocked and ready, Quirk asked the man to lay down his arms. The man screamed and charged in bloodlust and Quirk shot him dead. When Quirk rolled the man over, he was just a boy all of sixteen.*

*In two months the war would be over.*

*There was no need for that boy to have died.*

*And there are no words to describe having your heart ripped out of your chest when you return home from the war to find your wife and child buried in the yard of where your home once stood.*

*Quirk felt the tears on his face and heard his own anguished voice as he cried in his sleep and shouted for the nightmare to end.*

Michael and Michele sat next to Red Scar around the campfire and watched and listened as the dog soldiers told stories in their native language.

"What are they saying?" Michael asked Red Scar.

"They are talking of the old days when they were all young men and boys," Red Scar said. "When this land belonged to us and we roamed it freely."

"What was it like when you were a boy?" Michele asked.

Stuffing his pipe, Red Scar said, "I was born in 1835 not far from what you now call the Rocky Mountains." He lit the pipe off a stick from the fire and puffed. "We spent the spring and summer hunting and trapping and the winter living off what we hunted. I was ten years old before I saw my first white man. He was what they called a mountain man, and he went up into the mountains to live. I never saw him again."

"Were you scared?" Michele asked.

"More curious than scared," Red Scar said. "We knew of the white man, of course. Of his great war many years earlier and of their expansion west, but they hadn't reached us yet, so we were more curious about them than anything else. What did they want and how much of it, were always the questions asked by our elders around the campfire. The white men I first saw were French traders interested in beaver pelts and grizzly bears. I learned to speak the French language from trading with them. Then English from the English traders who followed the Dutch. It wasn't until after your second great war that they came in great numbers and our own numbers were reduced."

"What do you mean reduced?" Michele asked.

"He means killed," Michael said.

Michele looked at Red Scar.

"Tomorrow I will send scouts west to search for Quirk," Red Scar said. "They are restless and in need of something to do besides play stickball."

"Can we go?" Michael said.

"I promised to keep you close by my side," Red Scar said. "We have to move the herd to new grazing. I promised Quirk I would care for them as well."

"Is it true what Mr. Quirk said? That you became friends because you got tired of trying to kill each other?" Michael said.

Red Scar puffed clouds of smoke from his pipe. "We pretended we wanted to kill each other, but we really didn't. There was no point to it, so it became a game played between two old warriors who no longer had a war to fight, other than a war of nerves. Instead we became friends, and we're the better for it. Now that's enough talk for tonight. We have to be up early to move the herd."

When Quirk opened his eyes to bright sunshine, he knew instantly that his fever had broken.

Frog was cooking breakfast in a fry pan, and the aroma of bacon sizzling set his appetite on fire.

"You're up," Frog said.

"And hungry."

"Fever's gone," Frog said. "It broke during the night."

"I had bad dreams all night," Quirk said.

"I know. You talked a lot. So, it's two days' ride to where you left your herd, or a day and a half if we don't sleep."

"I'm not sure how strong I am just yet, but tie my hands to the saddle and I'll make it in a day and a half," Quirk said.

"Day and a half it is," Frog said. "Come eat some breakfast."

As they ate, Quirk said, "The law will be after you, Frank Miller's fault or not."

"I know," Frog said. "Frank was wrong, but I went along with him. That makes me wrong. Reckon I'll get three to five in Yuma for my part in it. Funny what men will do for their pot of gold."

"A man saves your life, you owe him a turnabout," Quirk said. "You have any money?"

"Some," Frog said. "Most is in Chicago, and I can't exactly walk into the bank and ask for it."

"I'll tell them I killed you with the others," Quirk said. "No one will question me. When we part ways, you go somewhere new and get yourself settled. Call yourself something else and send me a wire in Colorado in a month. Mention 'frog' so I know it's you, and I'll wire you a thousand dollars to any bank you want for a new start."

"That's a lot of money," Frog said.

"Breathing is worth more than money," Quirk said.

★ ★ ★ ★ ★

# Omaha

★ ★ ★ ★ ★

# Thirty

They moved the herd five hundred yards east to new grass beside a flowing stream of cold, clear water.

Michael and Michele rode with Red Scar and were not only able to keep up, but were quickly becoming excellent drovers.

Michael's hands were hard and calloused by now, and Michele's hands were no longer blistered or soft.

Odd as it sounded, they were proud of their rough, hardened hands and dirty fingernails.

Shortly before noon, while several of Red Scar's soldiers made a campfire to roast the chickens and rabbits they'd trapped, the twins joined a game of stickball and played on Red Scar's team.

At one point during the game one of the soldiers got carried away and tripped Michele during a pass. Red Scar flew into a rage. Driving his right shoulder into the soldier's stomach, Red Scar flipped him over his shoulder, and the soldier landed flat on his back. As a warning to the soldier, Red Scar placed his right foot on the soldier's neck and scolded him in Algonquian. The twins couldn't understand one word Red Scar said, but they got the general idea of who was the boss, and the boss wasn't happy. The game ended and everybody sat.

It was at that moment they heard a shot fired in the distance.

In his weakened condition, Quirk couldn't keep up with Frog on the marathon ride to catch up with the herd. Quirk felt his mind drifting and he fought hard to stay focused, but several times he felt himself pass out in the saddle. He'd awaken with a jolt and be unaware of where he was for a few moments. Then he would remember.

After nightfall Quirk fell asleep in the saddle and nearly fell off his horse, so Frog stopped long enough to tie Quirk's horse in tow.

By dawn, Quirk was somewhat awake and Frog was exhausted. They stopped once to eat some jerky and drink water, and Frog checked the ground for signs the herd had passed through.

The grass had been heavily grazed. The remains of a large campfire told Frog Red Scar and the children were no more than four hours ahead of them. Tracks of thirty or more horses pointed east in the direction of Omaha.

Frog mounted up, took hold of the tow rope, and pressed onward.

Hours later, with the hot noon sun beating down on them, Frog spotted smoke about a thousand yards in front of them. He stopped and looked at Quirk. The cowboy had either passed out or fallen asleep again. Frog couldn't tell which, but it didn't matter much now.

Frog dug his binoculars out of the saddlebags and scanned the horizon. From a thousand yards' distance the binoculars weren't powerful enough to see details, but he could make out Quirk's herd and a large group of people around the campfire. The people, he believed, were Red Scar and his band.

Frog put the binoculars away and then released Quirk's tether. He looked at Quirk for a few seconds and then touched a finger to his hat.

"*Adios,* cowboy," Frog said.

He turned his horse around, trotted about a hundred feet,

drew his gun, and fired one shot into the air.

The shot echoing across the plains stunned the band around the fire into momentary silence.

Red Scar was first on his feet. Within seconds all the soldiers, Michael, and Michele were standing and looking in the direction of the shot.

"I don't see anything," Michele said.

After the longest while scanning the horizon, Michele shouted, "There? See it? There. I see something."

"Where?" Michael said. "I don't see anything."

"A tiny speck of something," Michele said. "See it?"

Michael concentrated and held his hands above his eyes to block out the glare of the sun. "Yes, I see it," he said.

"I see it, too," Red Scar said. Then he spoke to his soldiers in Algonquian, and twenty of them went to their horses.

Michael and Michele were about to walk to their horses when the remaining ten soldiers surrounded them.

Red Scar mounted his horse and looked at the twins.

"No," he said.

Red Scar led his men out to the field. He started at a trot. As he grew closer to the speck on the horizon, he could see the speck was a man on horseback. As the gap narrowed, Red Scar recognized the man on horseback as Quirk, and he upped the trot to full-out run.

Surrounded by the soldiers, Michael and Michele couldn't see very much. Red Scar and his soldiers grew smaller and finally they, too, were tiny dots on the plains. After a while the dots stopped moving. Then they started moving again and slowly grew larger as they came closer.

When Red Scar and his soldiers were about a hundred yards away, the twins could see what Red Scar held in tow.

And they burst through the soldiers surrounding them and ran as fast as they could to Quirk. He was awake, but appeared weak, and his hands were tied to the saddle horn.

From the saddle, Quirk smiled at the twins.

"You two look like you could use a bath," Quirk said.

Shirtless, Quirk sat against his saddle while Red Scar's medicine man inspected the bullet wound on Quirk's abdomen. The cauterized skin was red and tender, but there was no sign of blood leakage or of the skin cracking open or infection.

Looking on, Red Scar said, "Maybe we should call you White Scar."

"Funny," Quirk said. "Almost as funny as getting shot in the belly."

"Hungry?" Red Scar asked.

"Yes."

"Rabbit stew in the pot," Red Scar said. "Put your shirt on and we'll eat."

They ate in a large circle. Red Scar sat to Quirk's right and the twins to his left. Quirk told them of the shootout with Frank Miller and how Frog saved his life.

"The herd looks well cared for," he said.

"I learned to drove," Michele said. She showed Quirk her blisters. "See?"

"Your aunt is going to love those," Quirk told Michele.

Quirk looked at Michael.

"And I suppose you're the new ramrod around here," he said.

"Mr. Red Scar is," Michael said.

Quirk looked at Red Scar. "Is that right?"

"One thing I don't understand," Red Scar said. "Why would this Frog save your life?"

"Sometimes when a man has done enough bad in his life, he

turns around," Quirk said. "I think that's what happened to him."

Red Scar nodded.

"Can we go to Omaha now?" Michael asked.

"It's five days' ride," Red Scar said to Quirk. "Can you make it?"

"I'll make it," Quirk said. "I got two new drovers and a new ramrod. All I have to do is not fall out of the saddle."

"So we'll start in the morning?" Michael said.

"On one condition," Quirk said. "That you take a bath tonight. And to tell you the truth, I could use one myself."

Red Scar looked at Quirk and sniffed. "To tell you the truth, I agree with you."

Four days later Quirk was nearly at full strength. He rode side-by-side with Red Scar and allowed the twins to run drover over the herd along with Red Scar's soldiers. They made a game of it to pass the time, keeping count of how many strays they could gather and add to the herd without breaking stride. Sometimes the twins took turns riding point to give the alpha bull something to follow.

"Amazing how far they've come in so short a time," Quirk said. "From eating candy to riding drover over a herd. From dresses to blisters."

"This country will grow you up quick," Red Scar said. "And old just as quick."

"Now don't go making us into old men just yet," Quirk said. "We got decades left in us, and I aim to make the most of them."

"I can always hope for another uprising," Red Scar said. "To add scalps to my collection."

Quirk grinned. "A man should have goals in life, I always say."

"Tomorrow we reach the army outpost at Omaha," Red Scar

said. "We will leave you before then."

"You'll do no such thing," Quirk said. "You'll ride in with me and resupply for the ride home. If the army doesn't like it, that's just too damn bad for them."

Around the campfire they feasted on wild turkey, beans, bacon, coffee, and condensed milk mixed with water. Supplies were low, but it didn't matter. Tomorrow they would reach the army outpost and restock for Red Scar's journey home.

"Colonel Curry is in charge," Quirk said. "He's a fine man and a good officer. He's probably wondering why I'm so late, but he won't hold it against me once he knows the story. His second in command is Captain Griffin. He handles the inventory and sets the price of beef and horses."

"I hope they have some candy," Michael said. "I sure could use a chocolate bar."

"They do, and a fine clothing store where we can get you and your sister some new clothes for the train ride home to Chicago," Quirk said.

Michele stood up, left the fire, and walked out to the field where the herd was grazing on grass under the setting sun.

Quirk looked at Michael. "Is she not feeling well?"

"She's upset about having to go home," Michael said.

"I see."

"Me, too, for that matter," Michael said.

Quirk stood up and followed Michele to the field. She appeared to be watching the herd, but was really shielding the mist in her eyes.

"What's bothering you, girl?" Quirk asked.

Michele didn't answer and lowered her head.

"Our parents are dead, my aunt doesn't want us, and we don't want to go to San Francisco to live with strangers," she said. "We want to stay with you on your ranch and be cowboys like you."

"With me?" Quirk said. "Oh, honey, I'm just an aging cowboy living in the middle of nowhere. You and your brother have your entire lives ahead of you, and if ever a pair was destined for great things, it's you two. Don't deny the greatness inside you because you're unhappy at the moment. The moment has a way of changing, and nothing will change it quicker than growing up proper."

"But our aunt doesn't love us, she doesn't want us, and we don't even know the relatives in San Francisco," Michele said.

"I am sure your aunt loves you very much and it was a hard decision to send you to San Francisco," Quirk said. "As for your relatives being strangers, we were strangers a short time ago, and look at us now. Sometimes you'll find if you give people a chance, they won't let you down. Thing is, without that chance, you'll never know."

Michele looked up at Quirk. He was so tall that when she hugged him, the best she could do was wrap her arms around his waist.

"Now I want you to do something for me," Quirk said. "When we ride into Omaha tomorrow, you keep your head up and look people in the eye. You never look away from nobody. Ever. Remember that and you'll be just fine."

# Thirty-One

The Corporal of the Guard at the Omaha Army Outpost couldn't believe his eyes when he spotted the herd on the plains a half mile out. From his vantage point on the twenty-foot-high catwalk, his field of vision was to the horizon, but he needed the powerful binoculars to see the details.

Stunned, he lowered the binoculars and looked down for a runner.

"Private!" he shouted.

The private, acting as the catwalk runner, rushed to the corporal's ladder.

"Yes, Corporal?"

"Better get Captain Griffin," the corporal said. "On the double."

Standing beside the corporal, Captain Griffin looked through the binoculars and said, "That's Matthew Quirk, all right. With two children and a band of dog soldiers. I'm not sure, but I think it's Red Scar leading them."

"Red Scar—who is he?" the corporal said.

"Before your time, Corporal," Griffin said. "Have the gate opened. I'm going to get the colonel and greet them."

Colonel Curry and Captain Griffin stood outside the open gates of the fort and watched as Quirk dismounted and walked to them.

"Better late than never at all, Colonel," Quirk said as he extended his hand and shook Curry's and then Griffin's.

"We just about gave up on you, Matt," Curry said.

"Had some trouble on the trail," Quirk said. "Bandits and kidnappers and such."

Curry looked past Quirk at the twins, Red Scar, and the dog soldiers. "This should make some interesting conversation at dinner," he said. He turned to Griffin. "Captain, considering all that Quirk has been through and the fact that we are in desperate need of fresh beef and horses, give him three and a half over prime rate for the cattle and one over prime for the horses."

"First things first, Colonel," Quirk said. "Let me get the cattle penned and the horses in the corral, and I got two youngsters that will need a bath and clean traveling clothes."

"Are those the Dunn twins?" Griffin said. "We had several wires they were missing from a train. I sent out several scouting details. Have they been with you the entire time?"

"Not quite."

"And Red Scar?"

"He and his men saved my life, you might say," Quirk said.

"Ask him if he would sit at my table," Griffin said.

"I will," Quirk said. "And by the way, I have a few wounds I'd like your sawbones to check."

Wearing a proper dress for dinner, Michele took her seat next to Michael. She appeared uncomfortable in the new clothes and felt oddly out of place.

Michael wore a suit with short pants and a tie that felt strange, even though he'd worn one every day to school since the age of five.

Quirk, clean-shaven and dressed in a black frock coat, white shirt, and thin tie, took the seat to Colonel Curry's right.

Red Scar sat at the colonel's left.

Captain Griffin and his junior officers occupied the rest of the seats at the very long table in the officers' dining hall.

"It's been a long time since I've seen you, Red Scar," Curry said.

"You were a captain then and I tried to shoot you with an old Hawken .50 caliber," Red Scar said. "It misfired, as they often did when the powder is damp."

"That was in 'seventy-three," Curry said. "I remember."

"I have a Winchester now," Red Scar said.

"Then I'm glad our warring days are over," Curry said.

"What time does the train in Omaha leave for Chicago tomorrow?" Quirk asked.

"Noon," Griffin said. "I wired their aunt as you requested. She'll meet you at the station in thirty-six hours."

Michael and Michele looked at Quirk.

"I'll be making the trip with them, Colonel," Quirk said. "I'd be obliged if you could livery my horse until I return."

"Not a problem," Curry said. He looked at the twins. "So, tell me about your adventures."

Quirk walked with Michael and Michele through the holding pens for the cattle to the large corral where Quirk's horse was one of many settled in for the night.

Quirk rested his arms over the fence, whistled softly, and his horse walked over and nudged his arms. Quirk gave him a few sugar cubes and rubbed his nose.

"Many of these horses the soldiers ride I brought in over the years," Quirk said.

Michele stood on a rung and rubbed the horse's neck.

"I suppose I'll be the only girl in private school in San Francisco who knows how to drover a herd," Michele said. "Or drive a chuck wagon, or find eggs on the prairie."

"When I was a boy in school, we had a show and tell day,"

Quirk said. "We'd bring something from home, show it to the class, and tell about it. Imagine what you two have to show and tell."

Michele rubbed the horse's neck a few more times and then stepped down beside Michael.

"Can we say goodbye to Mr. Red Scar?" she said.

"You bet," Quirk said. "If you don't, I'll never hear the end of it."

★ ★ ★ ★ ★

# Chicago

★ ★ ★ ★ ★

# Thirty-Two

As the train approached Chicago, Quirk was impressed with the changes the city had undergone since he last visited many years ago.

The skyline from a distance was large and imposing, with many tall buildings. As the train neared the station, the city seemed overpowering in its size and scope. Construction appeared to be everywhere, with old buildings being torn down to make way for newer, taller buildings.

Seated opposite them, Quirk looked at the twins.

"Michael, now is as good a time as any to say a few things about being a man," Quirk said. "Find out what you care about in life, and always stand up for what you believe in. Pick your friends for the right reasons and not because they're popular. Mind your manners and give respect to those who deserve it. Be independent in your life. Don't rely on anybody else for your happiness and success, or you'll resent it later on. Do the right thing and if you don't know what that is, just listen to the little voice in your head. He's never wrong. I make no claim to be a Thomas Edison, but those simple rules have never let me down. Okay, son?"

With mist forming in his eyes, Michael nodded.

"What about me?" Michele said. "Do you have any rules for me?"

"Just one," Quirk said. "Always and forever, you be the lady you are right now, and you will never let yourself or anybody else down. A real lady is a difficult thing to find in this world, and you are the genuine article if I ever saw one."

Michele started to cry, but Michael stopped her by taking her hand and giving it a good squeeze.

Quirk looked out the window as the train slowed. "We have arrived."

When the train stopped, Quirk and the twins went to a door.

"It appears our journey together has come to a successful conclusion," Quirk said.

The door opened and they stepped onto the platform. More people were rushing about than lived in the entire towns of Medicine Bow or Cheyenne.

Quirk took Michele's right hand.

"Let's find your aunt," he said.

As they walked along the very long and crowded platform, Michael took Quirk's left hand. They walked to the end of the platform and entered the very large station building.

"There," Michael. "By the information window."

Angela Dunn was a fine-looking woman, dressed in the height of Chicago fashion. When she spotted the twins, her face lit up in a dazzling smile of joy and relief.

Quirk led the twins to her.

"Miss Dunn, I'm Mathew Quirk," Quirk introduced himself.

Angela stared at Quirk for a moment, and the smile slowly disappeared. "I fully intended to have a US Marshal waiting to arrest you upon your arrival for endangering the lives of two children, but after receiving the entire story from the police and county sheriff, I decided not to pursue the matter," she said. "You may go on your way without consequence."

"Aunt Angela, Mr. Quirk saved—" Michael said.

"There is a carriage waiting outside with our driver," Angela said. "Please wait for me there. And for goodness sake, release Mr. Quirk's hands."

Michele stared at Angela for several long moments.

"No, we won't," Michele finally said.

"What did you say to me?" Angela said, somewhat shocked at the girl's tone.

"Mr. Quirk will walk us to the carriage," Michele said defiantly. "And that's all there is to it."

Holding Quirk's hands tightly, Michael and Michele led Quirk to the exit doors and outside to the street.

Speechless, Angela watched them walk away and then followed. She stopped at the doors and looked out through the glass.

Quirk stood over Michael and extended his right hand to the boy. They shook, and then Michael hugged Quirk tightly around the waist. When they broke apart, the boy's eyes were filled with tears.

Then Quirk got down on one knee and looked at Michele. She was openly crying. He hugged her tightly, and she wrapped her arms around his neck. He patted her back and then stood up and watched as the twins boarded the carriage.

With a final wave, Quirk turned and walked back into the station.

He paused and looked at Angela.

"If those kids were mine, I'd never let them out of my sight, much less give them away," he said. "But you do what you want, Miss Dunn."

Angela thought she detected a slight quiver in Quirk's voice and saw the mist in his eyes.

She wanted to say something to him, but he turned and walked to the platform to wait for the next outbound train and was soon lost in the crowd.

★ ★ ★ ★ ★

# Colorado

★ ★ ★ ★ ★

# Thirty-Three

Winter came late and left early. By late March, Quirk's reserve herd of fifty cattle had nearly doubled in size. His branded horses in the flats and valley numbered about a hundred, and in May he would round them up and the cattle and herd them to pasture for the spring grass to fatten them up for the next drive.

He received a wire from Frog in late November. He had settled in a small mining town in northern California. Quirk wired him a bank draft for one thousand dollars as promised. A month later, Quirk received a handwritten letter from Frog telling him he was now in the mining business and romancing a woman who ran a shop in town who didn't seem put off by his eyes one bit. They would probably be married and he would live out his days fat and happy.

He also received two letters from the twins. The first came just before Christmas and must have taken some time to write, because it was eleven pages long and written in black ink. The children's aunt placed them in a special private school for the winter, and a decision wouldn't be made until spring about sending them to San Francisco. They would turn thirteen in early February. They wished him a merry Christmas, and told him how much they appreciated and missed being with him.

Quirk folded the letter carefully and placed it between the pages of his wife's favorite passage in her Bible.

The second letter arrived at the end of March, and it was even longer than the first. The twins wrote of activity at school, of new things they had learned, including how to use the telephone and electric light bulb. Each was allowed to join a riding academy outside the city limits where on weekends they would practice their riding skills. They joked that they even managed to get their aunt to ride a horse or, more accurately, just to sit sidesaddle on one.

Quirk folded and placed the second letter with the first.

With the snow gone and the days warming up, Quirk was able to make repairs to the cabin, the corral, and barn that he'd put off all of last year.

At the end of April he rode to Denver for some equipment and wired Colonel Curry to notify him that in early September, he would drive a herd of several hundred cattle and a hundred head of horses to the fort in Omaha.

While in Denver, he purchased a new chuck wagon and new shingles for the roof. He started that task in May.

And on a fine afternoon in mid-May, Quirk was on the roof of his cabin replacing shingles when he spotted a carriage coming down the road toward his ranch. Shirtless, drenched in sweat, Quirk paused to drink from his canteen and watch the carriage grow closer.

And when he saw the carriage was occupied by the twins, and with Angela Dunn piloting the reins, Quirk felt something stir in his heart that had been missing since his wife and baby passed.

He came down off the roof and walked quickly to meet the carriage as it rode onto his property.

Michele didn't wait for the carriage to stop, but jumped down and ran into his arms. Michael wasn't far behind and, after a hug, Quirk received a warm handshake from the boy.

"Why didn't you write you would be coming?" Quirk asked.

"We're on the way to San Francisco and wanted to visit," Michael said. "And for it to be a surprise."

The carriage stopped. Quirk walked to it and took Angela's hand as she stepped down. She wasn't dressed in fine Chicago clothes, but wore riding pants with a blue denim shirt that made her appear younger and full of life.

"Do we always greet guests without a shirt on, Mr. Quirk?" Angela said.

"I do when I'm working on the roof and they aren't expected," Quirk said. "And call me Matthew."

"All right, Matthew," Angela said.

"I have to say, Miss Dunn, that this is a truly unexpected surprise," Quirk said.

"I've sold the house in Chicago, and we are moving to San Francisco," Angela said. "And call me Angela."

"All right, Angela," Quirk said.

"So this is your ranch," Angela said. "Matthew."

"And I have two guest rooms not in use, Angela," Matthew said.

"Is that an invitation, Matthew?" Angela said.

"Unless you want it in writing," Quirk said. "Angela."

"Tell him, Aunt Angela," Michael said.

"Tell me what?" Quirk asked.

"You're invited to come see us in San Francisco," Michele said. "Aunt Angela bought a farmhouse in the country."

Quirk looked at Angela. "Is that true, Angela?"

"Yes. So what is your answer, Matthew?" Angela said. "Will you come see us at our farmhouse?"

Quirk looked at Angela, and he saw the tiny smile on her lips and amusement in her eyes.

"Count on it," he said.

"Good," Angela smiled.

"Well, it's getting close to suppertime," Quirk said. "I best get washed up and put on a clean shirt."

"Can you cook, Matthew?" Angela said. She looked at the

twins. “Or should we help him with dinner?”

“How long can we stay, Aunt Angela?” Michele asked.

Angela looked at Quirk. “Better ask the cowboy that one,” she said.

# ABOUT THE AUTHOR

**Ethan J. Wolfe** is the author of many historical western novels and short stories. He has traveled the west and studied extensively, so his novels and short stories have a true western sense of realism.

The employees of Five Star Publishing hope you have enjoyed this book.

Our Five Star novels explore little-known chapters from America's history, stories told from unique perspectives that will entertain a broad range of readers.

Other Five Star books are available at your local library, bookstore, all major book distributors, and directly from Five Star/Gale.

Connect with Five Star Publishing

Visit us on Facebook:
https://www.facebook.com/FiveStarCengage

Email:
FiveStar@cengage.com

For information about titles and placing orders:
(800) 223-1244
gale.orders@cengage.com

To share your comments, write to us:
Five Star Publishing
Attn: Publisher
10 Water St., Suite 310
Waterville, ME 04901